The Private Life of Sherlock Holmes

The Private Life of Sherlock Holmes

By

MICHAEL and MOLLIE HARDWICK

From the Screenplay by
Billy Wilder and I. A. L. Diamond

Based on the characters created by
Sir Arthur Conan Doyle

IAN HENRY PUBLICATIONS

© Copyright
Michael & Mollie Hardwick, 1970

First published by Mayflower Books, 1970
Library edition published by Ian Henry Publications, 1975
Reprinted 1993

ISBN 0 86025 277 9

Produced by
Ennisfield Print & Design
Telfords Yard, 6-8 The Highway, London E1 9BQ
for
Ian Henry Publications Ltd.
20 Park Drive, Romford, Essex RM1 4LH

The Private Life of
Sherlock Holmes

CHAPTER ONE

THE MAN FROM CANADA

THE bank porter swung open the bronze-framed door of heavy glass for the woman to leave. The roar of the Hyde Park Corner traffic surged in, topped by the whistle and rumble of a big jet, letting down for Heathrow. The woman, still trying to wedge her wallet into an overfull handbag, thanked the porter. He gave her his severe little nod, civil but not obsequious, and closed the door behind her as she hurried away towards Piccadilly.

The decibels fell to a muted murmur. The porter resumed his stance, hands clasped behind him, feet firmly planted a few inches apart, chest out, head up, chin in: an old soldier, soldiering on in the phoney war of life.

One day, he told himself as he gazed out upon that vehicular whirlpool, all that lot'll stop. By the law of averages. One day, there'll be this almighty blooming jam along Knightsbridge; then this other up Park Lane, and it'll only want some clever devil to jump the lights at Piccadilly Circus or Marble Arch, and find he's half-way across and can't get forward or back, and that'll be it. They'll be snarled up from here to Victoria, along Knightsbridge and all Kensington to Notting Hill, and right through Mayfair to Oxford Circus one day.

He admitted other customers automatically, his train of thought uninterrupted. They'll be so stuck, they'll use loudspeakers from helicopters to tell 'em to leave their cars and walk home for the night, but be back at nine in the morning, sharp. That's a good one: nine to five in your car every day, waiting while some joker at Scotland Yard works it out on a map. And the blooming wardens giving tickets to everyone turning up late to sit in the jam.

Stimulated by the sight of a nervous motorist – a provincial, without a doubt – hesitating to change lanes and causing a momentary build-up of transport vehicles, taxis and the afternoon convoy of six No. 9 buses behind his wavering Morris 1100, the porter enlarged upon his fantasy. The Commissioner of Police, he'll say, 'There's a bloody great car transporter right across the mouth of New Bond Street. Get a spanner and go and take it to bits, and that'll let 'em start filtering left from Oxford Street.' 'Yes, Commissioner, sir. What do we do with the bits?' 'That's the driver's responsibility. He's in charge of the vehicle. If he obstructs the pavement with 'em, do him under Section 17b.'

Without disarranging his features the porter chuckled inwardly. I just hope it happens before March '73. Odds on it will, with another million or two of 'em on the roads. After that I shan't be standing here watching traffic. I'll have the weight off my feet in the old back parlour; or, better still, the front snug at the Lord Nelson.

A red sports car, driven by a young woman nipped between two taxis, cut out a Jaguar, and went dancing off towards the Piccadilly underpass. The porter was starting to work up a promising new fantasy when his attention was claimed by a youngish man walking slowly past the front of the bank: sauntering casually, yet peering intently towards the glass door as if trying to see into the recesses of the hall. Not that there was anything especially striking about the man. He would be in his late thirties; good carriage; fresh, clean-living looking sort of chap. Not English. American: you could always tell them from their coats and those hard little trilbies with a black band. There was an air-travel bag slung over his far shoulder, the porter noticed, as the man came into sight again, to pass the bank once more, peering in still and giving a glance at his watch as he went. AIR CANADA it said. Ah well, same thing. They all look the same.

No, there was nothing distinctive about this stroller: except that the porter had noticed him alight from a taxi some minutes earlier a little distance down the road.

Well, it was a free country still. You could walk up and down outside a bank or anywhere else all day if it suited you. Or he could be waiting for someone, though in all the porter's experience he couldn't remember anyone else choosing this noisy, windswept bit of London for a meeting place.

He made these observations and thought these thoughts unconsciously. As a bank porter, selected for your ex-Service record, you weren't paid just to open and shut a door. You were to keep your eyes peeled for the wrong 'un, who, like the shell with your number on it, might one day come exploding out of the blue.

The young man had stopped. He examined his watch, hitched the bag strap over his shoulder, and came towards the door. As he did so his right hand went down and he unzipped the little bag.

The porter hesitated fractionally before swinging open the heavy door, watching as the man's hand went down into the bag. He stood firmly, his uniformed body blocking entry as he asked, 'Can I help you, sir?' The man withdrew his hand from the bag.

'Excuse me.' The woman's voice came from behind the porter's back, startling him. His head turned and his eyes flickered away from the man. An elderly lady, smiling sweetly, was waiting for him to let her pass. With a quick nod to her he flicked his eyes back to the man, whose hand was extended towards him, holding a visiting card.

For one second precisely the porter stood motionless. Then the forgotten roar of traffic penetrated his ears again. He stepped aside and held the door for the woman, who thanked him and gave another of her delightful smiles to the other man, as he stood aside to let her pass and gave her a courteous North American-style inclination of the head. She crossed the pavement from the bank, her hand automatically raising into the kind of gesture royalty make from the carriage window. A taxi swooped to a halt beside her. With a single word to the driver, and a beaming smile, the little old lady got in and whisked away into the maelstrom.

The porter turned to the man at his side.

'Yes, sir?'

'Will you give this card to the manager, please?'

'The manager's clerk, sir, certainly. This way, sir.'

He marched stiff-legged to the far end of the glassed-in counter, stamped his hand imperiously upon a bell, and conjured up a middle-aged woman, who took the card and adjusted the spectacles dangling from a chain round her neck.

'Gentleman for the manager,' the porter announced, gave the man his little nod, turned on his heel and marched back to his post, to begin a new daydream about a perfectly timed conspiracy between a sweet little old lady and a man with an air travel bag and an ammonia spray.

The woman released herself from behind the counter by raising a flap.

'Have you an account?'

The man shook his head.

'No I don't.'

'But it was the manager you wished to see?'

'Mr. Havelock-Smith.'

'The managing director. I don't recall the appointment.'

'I don't have one. He wrote to me and said if ever I was this way back ...'

'I see. Well, I'll try; but I'm afraid, without an appointment ...'

Shaking her head and reading the visiting card again, she knocked at a tall, panelled door and entered, closing it behind her, leaving the man to gaze round the bank hall, watch the stream of people to and from the counters and read notices about interest rates on deposit accounts and the desirability of adding yet another type of credit card to the pack which nowadays demanded more wallet-space than what used to be known as money.

The managing director's room (no one ever termed it his office) befitted premises which stood within yards of No. 1, London – Apsley House, built for the great Duke of Wellington. It was oak-panelled: the panelling had been bought for a song by the banking group from the boardroom of an old-established business which, with professions of regret, it had forced into liquidation around the turn of the century. The fine fireplace had originated at the same source; the leather chairs, vast desk, books and other appurtenances of what resembled a library sitting-room had come out sheer profits. The impression was one of an oasis of serenity, serious-mindedness and intense application to vital affairs amidst the clanging frenzy of London in the seventies.

Mr. Havelock-Smith was just holing a ten-yard putt at the seventh at the Royal Sandwich when Miss Hopper's knock and entry jerked him back to Hyde Park Corner and consciousness. He was not surprised to find himself pacing his room with the measured tread and judicious droop of chin which his staff and visitors took for the depths of concentration. He was seventy and he had heard it all before. If he were to sit down and try to pay attention he would be snoring within two minutes. He knew it, and kept on the move.

Miss Hopper stood inside the door with a visiting card in her hand. Havelock-Smith raised a finger, adding a little smile of apology to the implied order to keep quiet until young Mr. Cassidy, of the legal department, had finished reading, and he, Mr. Havelock-Smith, had finished fixing his deepest concentration upon, a document of extreme length and tediousness.

'... in consideration of which, we (the bank) agree to extend to the aforementioned corporation a short-term credit of one million pounds, at a fixed interest rate of eight per cent per annum, to be repaid in four equal half-yearly instalments, beginning on 15th January, 1971.'

Mr. Cassidy read undeniably well. The jargon of commerce and finance was to him more musical than the cadences of Keats, more sonorous than the roll of the Old Testament. For him, one million pounds was no mere string of numerals, but a *million pounds* – stacked ingots in subterranean strongholds, notes receding end-to-end into infinity, a city block, a fleet of ships.... One million pounds was not a figure to be read out casually, a phrase to be thrown away, any more than the bank's magnanimity in making it available should be dismissed with slurred diction and a falling away of the voice on the drama implicit in that fateful '15th January, 1971'.

But the best readers indicate their paragraph endings with a pause, and Mr. Cassidy was no exception. Before he could draw breath to modulate into the minor key of the section outlining the conditions of granting the loan, Miss Hopper had nipped in like an obtrusive piccolo.

'A gentleman would like to see you, sir.'

Cassidy glanced up with a frown. Thankful for the diversion, Havelock-Smith reached out a hand, but caught his junior's glance and merely took the card without looking at it.

'Not now, Miss Hopper,' he sighed.

As Miss Hopper turned to the door she heard the performance resume.

'Paragraph Seven. As *collateral* for the aforesaid loan (suspenseful pause) the corporation shall transfer to the bank 40,000 shares of Class A non-voting stock ...'

'Just a moment.'

Thwarted in mid-climax, Cassidy broke off. Miss Hopper turned inquiringly. To the astonishment of both, their chief was transformed from a grave old banker with the weight of millions in bullion, notes and small change upon his shoulders to an eager-eyed, pinkly beaming gentleman who was hurrying to the door to fling it open wide and call into the bank hall beyond, 'My dear sir, come in, come in!'

He returned at once, ushering in the evidently surprised man with the flight bag, who was attempting to say something regretful about disturbing a busy man.

'Not at all, not at all. Fortunately, I happened to glance at your card. Thank you, Miss Hopper.' As his surprised secretary went out, he drew the stranger across to Cassidy, who had risen inquiringly to his feet.

'This is Mr. Cassidy, of our legal department. Cassidy, *this* is Dr. Watson.'

'Dr. ....?'

'Dr. Watson is the grandson of *the* Dr. Watson.'

The visitor extended a hand.

'How do you do, Mr. Cassidy?' The handshake was returned with evident uncertainty. Havelock-Smith said, with a hint of impatience, 'You *know. Holmes* and Watson. Baker Street.'

It registered at last, though Cassidy appeared no more fulfilled with the knowledge than without it. Dr. Watson was fishing in his bag, and this time brought out a rather crumpled letter.

'Mr. Havelock-Smith, I got this letter from you. About a tin box that belonged to my grandfather. I've been hesitating to walk in like this, only . . .'

'Quite right to do so, Dr. Watson. Yes, the box was left in our safe-keeping with the proviso that it must not be handed over to his heirs until fifty years after his death. Our records show that that period has now elapsed, and as we had your name as nearest surviving kin . . .'

'That's right. Say, though, I wonder what the old boy wanted to hide away like that?'

Havelock-Smith rubbed his hands.

'To tell you the truth, I've been rather curious myself. I, er, are you proposing to examine the box?'

'That's it.'

'Here?'

'Why not?'

'Splendid, splendid! You, er, won't mind if I . . .'

Dr. Watson laughed and allowed the older man to help him off with his coat.

'I wouldn't disappoint you like that.'

Havelock-Smith almost skipped as he turned to Cassidy.

'Call down to the vault, will you, and ask them to bring up the dispatch box marked "Watson"? It's in the old strong-room.'

Regretfully laying his papers aside, Cassidy moved away to a telephone on the managing director's acreage of desk. Havelock-Smith motioned the visitor into one of the leather chairs and crossed to a cabinet, which he unlocked with a small key on his chain.

'So, Dr. Watson, you're living in Canada?'
'Saskatchewan.'
'And practising medicine, just like your grandfather.'
'Well, actually I'm a veterinary surgeon. That's how I chanced to be here now. We're having a convention in London on foot and mouth disease, and I thought that while I was in England so soon after your letter...'
'Perfect. Sherry?'
'Please.'
Havelock-Smith poured a pale dry sherry from an antique decanter into two crystal glasses.
'You must be proud of your heritage, Doctor. To bear such an illustrious name...'
The younger man laughed and shook his head.
'Frankly, I've considered changing it to Jones or Brown.'
Havelock-Smith paused, the decanter suspended.
'What?'
'Nobody would think of saying "Elementary, my dear Jones" or "Elementary, my dear Brown." But if your name happens to be Watson, well, you can imagine.'
The banker, smiling again, handed him his sherry.
'Bit of a nuisance? To you, perhaps; but to me, it's poetry.' He closed his eyes and stood over the seated man, his drink untasted in his hand, and declaimed:
' "The gleam of the match which he struck shone upon the ghastly pool which widened slowly from the crushed skull of the victim. And it shone upon something else which turned our hearts sick and faint within us – the body of Sir Henry Baskerville!" '
He opened his eyes, to find the younger man staring at him.
'I beg your pardon, sir?'
It was the banker's turn to show surprise.

'Surely, Doctor! *The Hound of the Baskervilles.* Chapter 12. "Death on the Moor".'

To his disappointment, the Canadian's only response was, 'Say, how about that?'

Havelock-Smith toasted him silently and took refuge in his drink, motioning to Cassidy, who had finished telephoning, to pour one for himself.

'Yes,' he resumed, after savouring the old sherry, 'it may interest you to know that I'm a council member of the Sherlock Holmes Society of London. We meet several times a year and discuss the sacred writings.'

'Is that sort of thing still going on?'

'More strongly than ever. We're getting new members all the time, many of them very young. I dare say it's partly in protest against that secret service chap – the one with the hairy chest. What's his number...?'

It was Cassidy who answered. 'You mean 007? James Bond?'

'That's the one. Not exactly my idea of a gentleman.'

Watson grinned at Cassidy.

'They were showing *Goldfinger* on the plane coming over. I rather enjoyed it.'

Cassidy's eyes gleamed.

'Did you? I saw it six times.'

Havelock-Smith turned to him in surprise. 'As Holmes said to Watson, Cassidy, I never get your limits. But I regard that sort of thing as trash. Cheap sensationalism. Totally witless. Berettas and ... and bare bosoms. Sports car with flame-throwers and booby-trapped attache cases. SMERSH! Give me a foggy night; a hansom cab drawing up to 221B Baker Street; a desperate knock on the door ...'

As if on cue, there was a loud knock at the door. It opened to reveal a uniformed porter escorting another who cradled in his arms a battered tin dispatch box of an early make. A heavy cord surrounded it, the knot sealed with red wax, and a key dangled from the cord. Havelock-Smith indicated his desk. The porter placed the box carefully on the tooled-leather surface and followed his companion out of the door.

Havelock-Smith put down his sherry glass and gazed at the old box with a mixture of awe and reverence. Watson, who had risen to examine it, was testing the security of the sealed cord. Cassidy grunted.

'Doesn't look much, does it?'

His chief gave him an eloquent glance. Watson straightened up.

'Do you really mind if I open it here?'

'Mind!' the banker exclaimed. 'Dr. Watson, I'm seventy years of age. Why do you think I stayed on here past the age of retirement? It is because I have been hoping not to miss this moment.'

'Well, then – here goes!'

With a quick jerk, Watson broke the seal. He removed the key and inserted it in the lock. Havelock-Smith bent near. Even Cassidy moved close as the key turned.

'Gently, please, Doctor,' the old banker whispered as Watson began to lift the lid.

The first thing noticeable when the box was opened was a curious odour, such as might hang about an old type of solid-fuel stove that has been allowed to go out for the winter with the ashes of some unspeakable substance still in it. At a nod of permission from Watson, Havelock-Smith reached in and gingerly withdrew a pipe.

'Holmes's pipe!' he exclaimed, in the tones of a man who has been the first to handle, for ten centuries, the undoubted jawbone of a saint. He sniffed the bowl, recoiled slightly and handed it to Cassidy, who examined it with distaste.

Havelock-Smith plunged in again and surfaced with a large magnifying glass, and then, with a cry that bore elements of ecstasy, a deerstalker cap.

'Dr. Watson ...' He turned, childlike in eagerness, to the Canadian, who was watching with amusement: 'Do you think...? Would you have any objection if I...?'

Watson shook his head. With a kind of whimper of anticipation, Havelock-Smith clapped the deerstalker on his own head, tugged it into place, and hurried across to a glazed bookcase to try to see his reflection. Cassidy looked at Watson, who grinned and delved for the first time into the box. His expression changed as he produced a clumsy, early model of hypodermic syringe.

'I guess this is what Holmes used for his cocaine shots.'

Havelock-Smith came scurrying back to see.

Watson examined the syringe for a moment, then laid it aside.

'The less said about that, the better,' he grunted, and fished again, this time catching a handful of faded brown daguerrotype pictures. Too excited to remember his manners, the old banker grabbed them from him and began to deal them on to his desk top like a hand of cards.

'I guess there is a family resemblance,' conceded Watson, as a stiff studio portrait of what was unmistakably his grandfather turned up. It was followed by one, equally artificial in pose, of Sherlock Holmes, hand on the back of a chair in which Watson was seated; then another, livelier in theme, of Holmes, shirtless and legs in skin-tight breeches in the rigid classic pose of a barefist pugilist.

'A notable amateur pugilist,' bubbled Havelock-Smith.
' "Not Mr. Sherlock Holmes!" roared the prize-fighter. "God's truth! how could I have mistook you? If instead o' standin' there so quiet you had just stepped up and given me

that cross-hit of yours under the jaw, I'd ha' known you without a question." '

He became aware of the others' interested regard, lowered the fists he had automatically clenched into a fighting guard, and muttered, 'McMurdo. *The Sign of Four.* Er, any more? Good Lord! What a collector's piece! Watson as an Army doctor. Fifth Northumberland Fusiliers.'

'On an elephant?'

'Yes, yes. In Afghanistan – where he was wounded by a Jezail bullet, either in the left shoulder or the right leg. There are two schools of thought.'

'A *what* bullet?'

'Jezail. A long musket used by the Afghans.'

'Is that so? Say, who's this?'

Havelock-Smith had dealt out a photograph of a large man, probably in his forties, wearing a morning coat, striped trousers and grey top hat, and holding, with evident satisfaction, the reins of a horse in what looked like the winner's enclosure at an important racecourse.

'Ascot,' contributed Cassidy, who cared for more than the poetry of a balance sheet.

'And that's undoubtedly Mycroft Holmes, Sherlock's elder brother,' added Havelock-Smith. 'A remarkable man. Sherlock Holmes regarded his detective powers as even greater than his own, but he'd neither the ambition nor the energy to use them.'

Watson smiled and held up a sheet of manuscript music. The old lawyer peered, frowning, at the inscription at its head:

'For Ilse von H., by S.H.'

'Looks like a composition by Holmes!' he exclaimed.

'Exceedingly rare if it is. But 'Ilse von H.' . . .? No, no, I can't place any such person from your grandfather's published narratives.'

Watson smiled. 'Well, that's all – except for these.'

He held up a thick pile of paper, bound with faded red ribbon. His hands quivering, the old banker took them.

'May I?'

'Of course.'

Old fingers fumbled in their haste to undo the knot.

'This is manuscript. Perhaps the original of some of those very accounts of Holmes's cases for the *Strand Magazine*. You're a rich man if they are. . . .'

His voice trailed off as he read hastily, snatching off several sheets at random as if to compare one with another. Then, his voice affected by some deep emotion, he reached out a hand to support himself against the desk edge and turned to the waiting Canadian.

'Dr. Watson . . . this material has never been published.'

Watson took the documents and glanced curiously at a page or two.

'Are you sure?'

'Positive. I know every word.'

'Really, sir,' Cassidy could not prevent himself remarking, 'you speak as though you'd discovered a new play by Shakespeare.'

The old man rounded on him with surprising sharpness.

'Shakespeare? A dilettante! It took him five acts to solve a murder case. No, no, gentlemen. Believe me, if these papers should shed new light on the enigma that is Sherlock Holmes, then this may prove to be the most important literary find since . . . since the Dead Sea Scrolls!'

For a moment the Canadian regarded the old man curiously, wondering, not for the first time, what it was in the English race from which he himself was descended that could transform a man of advanced age and not a little importance from authoritative reserve into the semblance, virtually, of an excited schoolboy – cheeks flushed pink, eyes dancing with anticipation and delight, every movement eager and unrestrained by considerations of dignity or self-importance; and all this from a cause that to any other nationality would appear trivial to the point of absurdity.

For a moment he felt himself moved to be at the centre of such a demonstration, and a part of the reason for it; but then the natural curiosity and ebullience of the North American swept sentiment aside, and, motioning the old banker and his assistant into two of their own chairs, he picked up the bundle of papers and began to read aloud: not in the declamatory style of Cassidy, nor with the dramatic delivery of Havelock-Smith, but in that quieter, more matter-of-fact way that carried with it to this hushed room in the heart of a seething London of the 1970s evocative echoes of a smaller, less frenetic, but still bustling capital of nearly a century before, and, had he known it, of the voice of a man who had resembled, in form and spirit, this grandson of his from a newer world.

CHAPTER TWO

A RACING ENGINE

IN my lifetime (*the manuscript began*) I have recorded more than sixty cases which demonstrated the singular gifts of my friend Sherlock Holmes, the best and wisest man who ever lived. But there were other adventures shared by us which, for reasons of discretion, I have decided to withhold from the public until a later date. They involve matters of a delicate and sometimes scandalous nature, as will become apparent to the reader when these papers are perused after the expiry of the stipulated term.

I record them here with no prurient intention, but in the sincere belief that by showing my friend to have been something other than the reasoning machine of popular legend, devoid of human emotion and immune to human weaknesses, I may manage to repair those omissions from my printed accounts which have hitherto troubled my conscience as biographer of a singular man.

(Then followed several paragraphs of instructions as to the eventual manner of publication of the manuscript, including an interesting suggestion that the rising medium of the kinematograph might be explored in this connection. The preamble closed with a succinct quotation from Sherlock Holmes's most admired philosopher and namesake, Oliver Wendell Holmes, upon the nature of human fallibility. The narrative then followed, in the form in which it is now printed for the first time.)

It was September of 1887, and Sherlock Holmes and I were returning to London from Yorkshire, where he had solved the mystery of the death of Admiral Abernetty. This, of course, was the case in which Holmes brought the murderer to book by proving that when the fatal shot was fired the short-sighted chambermaid had been looking not at a clock whose hands pointed to 11.55, but at a barometer indicating 29 degrees of pressure and prolonged outbreaks of rain.

We had travelled through the night and drove wearily and in silence through the early-thronging streets of London. We exchanged no word throughout the length of the Euston Road and Marylebone Road; but as we turned into Baker Street it was as if we were suddenly refreshed and we chatted animatedly. Such was the invariable effect upon both our spirits of any return to No. 221B, an address which, however much associated in the popular mind with murder, blackmail and countless other misdeeds, to us was simply home.

It was pleasant, that morning as always, to mount those seventeen stairs, and comforting to find at their head our welcoming landlady and housekeeper, Mrs. Hudson: kindly, patient, cheerful in the face of Holmes's incurable untidiness and thoughtless eccentricities, although, to my mind, she regained not a little compensation by the amount she charged us for our quite modest quarters.

We had not been long gone, but it was as reassuring as ever to gaze upon the dear clutter of our sitting-room, the starting-point of so many remarkable expeditions and adventures; the midnight confessional for countless visitors of both sexes, perplexed, distressed, terror-stricken, with their bizarre tales of injustice, fear and every species of human folly.

The fire was burning brightly and a cheery warmth enveloped us as we removed our travelling clothes. Beside the fireplace stood the coal scuttle, containing, along with the fuel, the customary box of cigars which more than once an absent-minded gesture by Holmes, when deeply absorbed in some problem, had nearly swept into the fire in mistake for a coal. The Persian slipper, receptacle for tobacco, lay in its place, reminding me for a distasteful moment of another slipper, monogrammed with a coat-of-arms, and the disagreeable events of earlier that morning. However, the mood was prevented from returning by the sight of the other trusty objects about me: Holmes's velvet-upholstered wing chair; the cushioned couch, which, if it could have spoken, could have repeated many strange tales told by those who had sat upon it; the basket chair with the special writing-arm in which I had penned so many of my accounts of our adventures together; the sideboard, with full tantalus and well-charged gasogene; the plain deal table, heavily acid-stained, bearing the chemical equipment with which Holmes was accustomed to fill our premises with abominable odours, and which, more than once, had been the means of experiments whose outcome would mean life or death for someone; our dining table, scene alike of snatched meals and epicurean feasts; our bookshelves, jammed with annals of ancient and modern crime and those bulky commonplace books with which Holmes supplemented the incredible store of miscellaneous knowledge accommodated in what he termed his 'brain attic'. There it all lay before and around me – Holmes's violin in its case, the oil lamps, the bell-pull: everything, in fact, which I have always sought to make as familiar a part of my narratives as the habits and characteristics of the remarkable man to whose Johnson it has been my privilege to play Boswell.

'You will find your letters on the mantelpiece, gentlemen,' Mrs. Hudson broke in upon my reverie. Beside the spot where Holmes habitually impaled unanswered correspondence to the mantelpiece with a jack-knife lay a small pile of mail containing one knew not what preliminary to some new investigation and perhaps danger.

'I do wish you would give me a little more warning when you're coming back unexpectedly,' Mrs. Hudson continued in the more querulous tone which it was her habit to adopt when some long-born irritation insisted upon being expressed. 'I would have roasted a goose and had some flowers for you.'

'My dear Mrs. Hudson,' Holmes replied, without turning from what he was doing, 'criminals are as unpredictable as colds in the head. You never quite know when you're going to catch one.'

Mrs. Hudson plainly shared my own astonishment at this unaccustomed display of pawky humour from my friend. The impetus effectively removed from her complaint, she could only say that she would unpack our bags, and go through to Holmes's bedroom.

I took down one of the envelopes from the mantelpiece and ripped it open.

'Holmes,' I cried with pleasure. 'Here is an advance* copy of the *Strand Magazine*. They have printed my account of the *Adventure of the Red-Headed League*.'

I held out the journal for Holmes's perusal. He made no attempt to take it from me.

'Would you care to see how I have treated it?' I insisted.

'I can scarcely wait,' he replied dryly, slicing his way into a letter of his own with a stiletto. 'You know my views about

---

*Very much in advance. The *Strand Magazine* did not begin publication until 1891, four years after the purported date of these events. This is clearly yet another instance of Watson's notorious inconsistency in the matter of dates.

your deplorable tendency to over-romanticize my activities. You have taken my simple exercises in logic and embellished them, embroidered them, exaggerated them....'

'I deny the accusation.'

'You have described me as six feet four in height, whereas I am barely six feet one.'

'Poetic licence.'

'You have assigned to me an improbable form of costume, which the public now expect me to wear.'

'That was not my doing, Holmes. You may blame that upon the illustrators of my narratives.'

'You have given me the reputation of a virtuoso of the violin.'

He thrust the opened letter at me.

'Just look at this: an invitation to appear as soloist in the Mendelssohn concerto with the Liverpool Philharmonic. The fact is that I could barely hold my own in the orchestra pit of a second-rate music hall.'

'You are too modest.'

He affected to ignore the compliment. 'You have given your readers the distinct impression that I am a misogynist. Actually, I don't dislike women: I merely distrust them. The twinkle in the eye, the arsenic in the soup....'

'It is precisely such colourful little touches that appeal to my readers so much,' I retorted.

'Lurid would be a better word. You have also painted me as a hopeless drug addict, on the strength of an occasional indulgence in a five per cent solution of cocaine.'

'Seven per cent, Holmes.'

'*Five.* You have been diluting it behind my back for years.'

He petulantly picked up his deerstalker hat and set it upon a porcelain phrenological head.

'Holmes,' said I, 'as a doctor, as well as your friend, I

strongly disapprove of this insidious drug habit of yours.'

'My dear friend, as well as my dear doctor,' he replied without sarcasm, 'I only resort to narcotics when I am suffering from acute boredom; when there are no interesting cases to engage my mind. Give me problems, Watson, activity, and you will see no syringe in my hand. The purpose of your habitual drug-taker is to escape: to find an excuse for inactivity. Mine is to overcome the frustration of having no activity into which *to* escape. Unfortunately, the days of the great criminals appear to be past. As to this little practice of mine, it appears to have degenerated into an agency for the recovery of lost midgets.'

'Lost *midgets*, Holmes?'

He waved a letter. 'Six of them. The Tumbling Piccolos – an acrobatic act with some circus. Disappeared between London and Bristol.'

'Intriguing enough for you, I should have thought.'

'Oh, extremely so. You see, they are not only midgets. They're anarchists.'

'Anarchists!'

'By now they will have been smuggled to Vienna, dressed as little girls in organdie pinafores. They are to greet the Czar of Russia when he arrives at the railway station. They will be carrying bouquets, concealed in each of which will be a bomb with a lit fuse.'

'Holmes!' I exclaimed. 'We must notify the authorities at once!'

'Not at all. The circus owner is offering me five pounds to find them. That is less than one pound per midget. Obviously, he is a tight-fisted employer and the little chaps have simply run off to join another circus.

'Forgive me, my dear chap,' he apologized, seeing my crestfallen countenance. 'But depend upon it, there are no great crimes any more. The criminal class has lost all enterprise and originality. At best they commit some bungling villainy with a motive so transparent that even a Scotland Yard official can see through it.'

He had wandered to his desk, piled with newspapers, memoranda and other seemingly haphazard documents. Suddenly, he spun on his heel.

'Mrs. Hudson!' he shouted.

Our landlady came hurrying from the bedroom, one of Holmes's soiled shirts in her hand.

'Mrs. Hudson, there is something missing from my desk.'

'Missing, sir?'

'Something very crucial.'

'I'm sure, sir, I can't think what.'

'Dust.'

He ran his finger along the desk top and wagged it at her.

'You have been tidying up against my explicit orders.'

'I made sure not to disturb anything,' Mrs. Hudson retorted hotly.

Holmes shook his head impatiently. 'Dust, Mrs. Hudson, is an essential part of my filing system. By the thickness of it I can date any document immediately.'

Our landlady gave an indignant snort and held up her forefinger and thumb, an inch apart.

'Some of the dust was that thick.'

'That would be March, 1883.'

The feud between Holmes and our landlady was renewed that same evening as Mrs. Hudson cleared our dinner dishes from the table. After the meal I had repaired immediately to my writing chair, to commence my account of our latest adventure together, while Holmes, to my dismay, had begun to assemble the latest device to capture his restless interest, his smoking machine. This loathsome contraption, which now stood on the deal table, consisted of a framework supporting a series of rubber tubes, in the end of each of which was inserted a cigarette, a cigar, or the mouthpiece of a pipe. A foot-pedal activating our old fire bellows caused the necessary process of inhalation and exhalation, and once the tobacco had been lighted, and the pedal got into brisk action, the room took little time to gain a resemblance to the innermost depths of a long railway tunnel on a day when excursion trains were frequent in both directions.

Holmes, in shirtsleeves, was pumping busily and collecting specimens of the respective ashes upon little glass slides, which he would then scrutinize under a microscope before making copious notes in a book. I was trying to see the page in front of me, and Mrs. Hudson, coughing harshly, was battling with her tray in the direction in which she had last seen the door.

'How can you stand this?' she suddenly exclaimed between paroxysms. 'Why don't you let me air the room out?'

'Ssh, Mrs. Hudson!' I warned her. 'Mr. Holmes is working on a definitive study of tobacco ash.'

'I'm sure there's a crying need for that,' was her retort.

'In our endeavours,' I explained, overlooking her pertness, 'it is sometimes vital to distinguish between, say, the ash of a Macedonian cigarette and that of a Jamaican cigar. So far, Mr. Holmes has classified one hundred and forty different types of ash.'

'Most of which,' she commented, 'has finished up on my rug.'

'That will be enough, Mrs. Hudson.'

'All right. If you gentlemen want to stay here and suffocate ...'

A spasm of coughing prevented her from finishing her sentence. She staggered blindly doorwards again, found it by chance, and vanished, her receding coughs resounding up the stair well.

For some moments the creak of the foot-pedal and the sigh of the bellows continued; then, all at once, they ceased, and the form of Holmes approached me through the murk.

'She's right, Watson. I *am* suffocating.'

'I can assure you I am,' I responded, rising. 'Let me open a window.'

'Not from lack of air, Watson: from lack of activity. Sitting here week after week, blowing smoke rings, staring into a microscope – there's no challenge in that.'

'Personally, I consider it a major contribution to scientific criminology.'

Holmes had found his violin case and opened it. He plucked moodily at the strings of his Stradivarius.

'How I envy you your mind, Watson.'

'You, Holmes?'

'It's placid, imperturbable, prosaic. But my mind rebels against stagnation. It is like a racing engine, tearing itself to pieces because it is not connected up with the work for which it was built.'

He thrust the fiddle under his chin and began to play. For all his protestations he played well, better than most amateurs and some professionals. I could not recognize the melody. He seemed to be improvising one of those nervous, pent-up tunes which boded no good for his well-being or for our relationship. I attempted to concentrate upon my manuscript, but was barely surprised when, after a few moments, Holmes laid down the violin, crossed swiftly to the sideboard, and, before I could protest, had opened my medical bag and plucked out a bottle of cocaine. I found my voice, but he paid no attention, passing on into his bedroom. I cast my papers aside and hurried after him. He had placed the bottle on his washstand and was already rolling up his left sleeve.

'Holmes! Where is your self-control?'

'A fair question,' was the grim reply.

From a shelf he took down the morocco leather case whose every appearance I had come to dread, and removed a hypodermic syringe.

'Aren't you ashamed of yourself, Holmes?'

'Thoroughly. This will take care of that.'

He had opened the bottle, inserted the needle, and was drawing up the fluid. For a moment, as so often before, I considered leaping forward to dash both syringe and bottle from his hand. As always, resolution deserted me. Much as I abominated the use of drugs for other than the alleviation of pain, I knew that they had their part to play in the unorthodox life of my strange companion. There was in his exceptional nature some deficiency, some lacking element, which only the drug habit, rather than the drug itself, could replace.

Then, before I could quell it, the bitter accusation had sprung unbidden to my lips.

'You value my companionship because it suits you to have a ready source of stimulants.'

'Do not underestimate your other charms, my dear fellow,' he answered with maddening indifference. 'By the way, I shall be grateful if you will replace this needle. It is getting rather blunt.'

I heard the parlour door open and saw Mrs. Hudson enter, carrying the tea tray. Holmes whipped the syringe guiltily out of sight behind his back.

'Mrs. Hudson,' I said, going out to her, 'I want you to pack my bags, please.'

'Certainly, sir,' she replied, setting out the tea things. 'For the week-end, or longer?'

'A great deal longer. I am leaving here.'

'Leaving?'

She glanced towards Holmes in his doorway. He merely shrugged.

'I am as surprised as you, Mrs. Hudson,' he affected to confess.

'As quickly as you please, Mrs. Hudson,' said I. She hesitated for a moment, then went through into my bedroom and I heard the sound of my valises being dragged from under the bed.

'Might one ask,' inquired Holmes, 'where you propose going?'

'I don't know. I shall resume my medical practice. I *am* a doctor, you know.'

'You'll find it very dull. Oh, if you are looking for your medical bag, it's under that chair – where you last hid it.'

I found the bag, set it on the table and opened it.

'I shall, of course, continue to pay my half of the rent until you find someone to share these rooms with you. Meanwhile, here is my farewell present to you, Holmes – a fresh needle for your syringe. And here are three full bottles of cocaine. If you wish to destroy yourself, pray do so. Don't expect me to sit by and watch you doing it.'

I placed the bottles in a row upon the mantelpiece, took up my bag and went through to my room to assist Mrs. Hudson with my packing, closing the door after me in what I intended to be a meaningful way.

To my intense surprise, Mrs. Hudson was crying to herself as she folded and packed my linen. Indeed, she was compelled to seize one of a pile of my freshly laundered handkerchiefs and blow her nose upon it.

'I'll wash it and send it on to you, Doctor,' said she with

difficulty. 'Oh dear me, it's so sad, you and Mr. Holmes, after all these years...'

I opened my other valise and commenced to pack my suits.

'Actually,' I assured her, hoping a cheerful front would restore her spirits, 'I'm rather looking forward to leading a normal life again: reasonably regular hours, and the likelihood that if I'm called out in the night it will be to an appendicitis* and not an axe murder. Henceforward, I'll leave the fog and sleet and the bloodstains to Holmes. . . .'

The word 'bloodstains' had barely left my lips when there came from the sitting-room the loud crash of a pistol shot. For a moment, Mrs. Hudson and I looked at one another, frozen in horror. Then followed another explosion. I ran to the door and wrenched it open.

To my relief, Holmes was seated at his desk, a smoking revolver in his hand. He was taking aim, not at his own head, but at the solitary survivor of the three cocaine bottles which I had placed upon the mantelpiece shortly before. The shattered remnants of the other two lay nearby, and a trickle of liquid ran down into the hearth.

'Mr. Holmes!' cried Mrs. Hudson indignantly. 'How many times have I said that I won't tolerate your indoor shooting?'

Holmes's answer was to squeeze the trigger yet again. There was a loud report, a scream from Mrs. Hudson, and then the tinkle into the fender of glass fragments from the third bottle.

'Outrageous!' our landlady shrieked.

---

* Watson had clearly been keeping up to date with the medical journals. Appendicitis had scarcely been known until 1886, the year before the events of which he is writing, and the name would not have sprung readily to the lips, even of a general practitioner, in casual illustration of a point.

'It's all right, Mrs. Hudson,' I reassured her, smiling. 'I'll tidy up the mess, while you unpack my things.'

'Of all the ... *Un*pack?'

'Exactly.'

With a stare and a shake of her head, the poor woman returned to my room. I took up the coal shovel and a little brush and began to collect the broken glass.

'Thank you, Holmes,' said I. 'I know how difficult the decision must have been.'

Holmes rose from his chair.

'Not at all, my dear fellow. A simple choice between a bad habit and a good companion.'

'You have made me very happy.'

'I have often been accused of being cold and unemotional, Watson. I admit it, and yet, in my cold, unemotional way, I'm very fond of you.'

'I know it,' I assured him, though one likes to hear these things said occasionally.

I noticed his violin lying on a chair near the fireside. It had been spattered with the flying fluid.

'Holmes,' I said, 'your Stradivarius. It must be wiped at once.'

I picked it up and made for his violin case, where I knew he kept the cloth with which he would occasionally rub up the varnish of his instrument. To my slight surprise he sprang across the room to intercept me, seizing a napkin from the tea tray as he moved.

'No, no, Watson, you are not to trouble yourself. Let me do it.'

He firmly removed the violin from my hands and rubbed it vigorously with the cloth. Then he carried it to the case, carefully laid it inside and snapped the case shut.

Looking back to the incident now, it is tempting to condemn myself for permitting so simple a deception to pass unperceived. I confess that the combination of his unaccustomed flattery and my gratification at the apparently successful outcome of a plan that had seemed to have failed took away my watchfulness and rendered my imagination impotent. Had it been otherwise, I should surely have tasted the liquid which had escaped from those shattered bottles, and found it water or some such harmless substance. Had I examined the fragments of the bottles themselves, I should no doubt have found them to have been of slightly different shape to my cocaine bottles. Doubtless, I should have found others like them amongst the chemical apparatus which bestrewed our room.

As Sherlock Holmes so often charged, I saw, but did not observe. Nor did I hear, as he would undoubtedly have heard if our roles had been reversed, the slight chink of bottles as he placed the violin in its case. I saw none of these incriminating details, heard none. My only ears were for the flattery of my friend, and my only eyes for the comfortable home in which, after all, I could remain.

CHAPTER THREE

THE SINGULAR AFFAIR OF THE RUSSIAN BALLERINA

In one of my previously published narratives I mentioned that Sherlock Holmes had acquired his violin from a pawnbroker in the Tottenham Court Road, for the sum of fifty-five shillings. To those who know the value of a Stradivarius, it will be obvious that I was being less than candid about the matter. The true story of how he came into possession of this fine instrument could not be disclosed until now without fear of tarnishing the good name of one of the most celebrated women of the time. What its reflection upon the characters of Holmes and myself would have been will be readily apparent from the following pages.

This nightmarish episode began one June morning in '85. Our breakfast table had not yet been cleared and the agreeable odours of coffee and bacon still hung upon the already warm air. Clad in my dressing-gown, I paced the floor of our sitting-room, holding in one hand a letter on blue stationery and in the other two theatre tickets which had been its enclosures. Through the open door of his bedroom I was addressing Holmes, who was taking his morning tub in a hip bath.

'Holmes, I can't understand your stubbornness. It is the final performance by the Imperial Russian Ballet; the house has been sold out for months; and yet, when someone takes the trouble to send us two complimentary tickets you simply refuse to go.'

'That is precisely why,' Holmes answered, plying the loofah. 'Ask yourself, Watson, what reason anyone could have for sending us the tickets – anonymously, too.'

'In anticipation of your help.' I referred again to the letter. 'It says here, "Please! You are the only man in the world who can help me."'

'Ha! I suspect it is some kind of plot.'

'A trap, you mean? Someone wishes to lure us into a trap?'

'Somebody wants to kill me.'

'*Kill* you, Holmes?'

'Bore me to death. It has come to their ears that I detest ballet.'

'But it is *Swan Lake*!'* I hummed a few bars from the *pas de deux*. 'Tschaikowsky at his most lyrical.'

'It's not the music. What nauseates me is the sight of muscle-bound nymphs being pursued by dainty young men in tights who look as though they would rather be chasing each other.'

'I allow you to drag me to all those dreary violin recitals ...'

'My dear Watson, why don't you just go without me?'

'And let the other ticket go to waste?'

Before he could reply the sitting-room door opened and Mrs. Hudson entered, carrying a blue envelope.

'This just came for Mr. Holmes. By messenger.'

'In here, Mrs. Hudson,' my friend called.

* It couldn't have been, in 1885. The first version of *Swan Lake* reached the Russian stage in 1877, proved a total failure and was not performed again, even in Russia, until 1895. Extracts only were seen in London, and not before the turn of the century; and the first full version was presented at Sadler's Wells in 1934. No Russian ballet company visited London until 1910 (Diaghilev's), and no Russian State ballet company until 1956 (The Bolshoi). Clearly, the dancer, not the dance, was what held Watson's attention.

By averting her eyes and assuming a crab-like sideways gait, Mrs. Hudson was able to deliver the envelope to Holmes in his tub. She retreated thankfully.

'Mrs. Hudson,' he called after her, 'how would you like to go to the ballet this evening?'

'The ballet, sir?'

'Dr. Watson will take you.'

She turned inquiringly to me.

'With pleasure,' I said.

'I've never been to the ballet, sir.'

'Then you're lucky to be going with an expert such as Dr. Watson. He will explain it all to you.'

Mrs. Hudson radiated positive excitement.

'What shall I wear?' she consulted me.

I strove to picture her in other than the familiar apron and household dress, but before I could make any suggestion Holmes called again: 'Get my dress suit out of mothballs, Mrs. Hudson.'

'Your dress suit? How will I look in your...'

'Not for you. The plans have been changed. I'm going with Dr. Watson myself.'

I observed that he had the letter open in his hand.

'What is it, Holmes?'

'See for yourself.'

I took the single sheet of blue notepaper. In the same handwriting as the invitation I read the single sentence: 'And don't send your landlady.'

To me, if not to my friend, that evening spelt enchantment. Our seats in a Stalls Circle box commanded a perfect view of one of the most famous stages in Europe. Around us, even in the dimmed light, the twinkle of diamonds and the gleam of magnificent shoulders and bosoms revealed the presence of more beautiful women than it had been my fortune to see for many a day, for Holmes's female clients tended to be on the homely side.

But not one of the stately devotees of ballet, jewelled and satin-clad in addition to their natural charms (a particularly pretty little creature in pink had bestowed several inviting smiles on me before the rise of the curtain), could compare with the woman who danced on that great stage. A simple, low-cut bodice outlined her excellent figure, a feathery tutu revealed a gratifying amount of her magnificent legs; a face of proud Slav beauty, framed in raven black hair, expressed all the sorrows of Odette the Swan Princess, imprisoned by magic within the form of a bird.

As for her dancing, surely London had never seen the like of it. *Tour en l'air, jeté, entrechat* – she performed them all with the most perfect grace and butterfly lightness. Perhaps, I reflected, she was a *shade* dark for my taste: whereas that delicious little cygnet, third from the left, with the winsome tiptilted nose ... but there was no doubt that Petrova's charms, allied with such technique, were utterly compelling.

'A fabulous woman, don't you think, Holmes,' I whispered, unable to take my eyes from the stage.

He stirred and grunted. 'Eh? Who?'

'The great Petrova.'

I forced my glasses upon my companion, who reluctantly focused them upon the dancer. After a moment's study he handed them back.

'Very strong arches, I must admit.'

'They say twelve men have died for her.'

'Really?' he yawned.

'Six committed suicide, four were killed in duels, and one fell from the gallery of the Vienna Opera House.'

'That makes only eleven.'

'The man who fell landed on one of the orchestra.'

I returned my attention to the charming spectacle. After some little while I heard the rattle of the rings from which hung the red plush curtain covering the door to our box. Glancing round, half expecting to see Holmes leaving, I was surprised to find my companion still at my side, also looking round at the man in evening clothes who stood regarding us from the box entrance. He was in his middle fifties and expensively dressed and groomed. His silvering hair was delicately waved and his short beard immaculately trimmed. My immediate impression was of someone both suave and sinister.

'Mister Holmes?' he inquired, in a grating voice and an accent unfamiliar to my ear.

'I am Holmes.'

'I am Nicolai Rogozhin, director-general of Imperial Russian Ballet.' He gave a sharp, stiff little bow. 'So glad you accept invitation.'

'Not at all. This is my friend and colleague, Dr. Watson.'

The Russian bowed again. 'So pleased to meet you.' He took one of the seats behind us. 'You are enjoying?'

'Immensely,' I responded warmly.

He nodded, seemed to hesitate for a moment, then addressed Holmes again.

'Tell me, Mr. Holmes, how is your health?'

'You had better consult my doctor.'

'He is in excellent shape,' I answered without bidding.

The Russian appeared gratified.

'No insanity in the family? Diabetes? Asthma?'

Holmes forestalled me with a gesture. 'Would you mind telling me what this is about?'

'Certainly. Madame Petrova, she has problem.'

'Would you be more specific?'

'Certainly not.'

'A liaison with a crowned head, perhaps? Compromising letters? Blackmail?'

Our visitor shook his head vigorously.

'More delicate than that. Much more.'

He rose to his feet.

'After performance will be small celebration on the stage. Madame request your presence.'

'We shall be delighted,' I said with enthusiasm.

He turned to me.

'You are invited, too.'

He whisked aside the curtain and made his departure. An alien perfume was left hanging upon the air. I glanced at Holmes who was staring at the movement on the stage.

'Strange fellow, Holmes. And what curious questions.'

Holmes reached across and took my opera glasses, which he trained upon Petrova, who was making her spectacular exit, moving rapidly backward towards the lake on twinkling points, amidst the start of a rousing ovation.

'Curiouser and curiouser,' I heard my companion murmur.

The scene backstage after the performance might almost have been an extension of the ballet itself for glitter and gaiety. The light twinkled upon serried ranks of bottles of vodka and champagne, the principals, as it were, of the performance about to begin, and on its *corps de ballet*, a host of gleaming glasses, slender and fragile as ballerinas and as promising of pleasure. Plates of caviar and other delicacies, silver cutlery, snow-white napkins lay before our gaze as Holmes and I entered from the wings and prepared to mingle with the throng of costumed dancers, other men and women like ourselves in evening dress and a handful of men in the more workaday clothing of stage technicians. Members of the orchestra were grouped together playing gypsy melodies on balalaikas. The air was a-buzz with laughter and the triumphant satisfaction that follows resounding success.

Rogozhin came hurrying towards us, motioning to a waiter.

'There you are, Mr. Holmes! Madame is expecting you in her dressing-room. Dr. Watson, you will amuse yourself meanwhile, yes? You see we have vodka, caviar, girls.'

'No thank you.'

'No girls?'

'No caviar.'

Rogozhin beamed, turned towards a chattering group of ballerinas and clapped his hands, calling in words incomprehensible to me, although I fancied I heard something corresponding to my name. Whatever it was, I was immediately surrounded by the bevy of little beauties and a glass of vodka was thrust into one of my hands and one of champagne into the other.

'Do any of you ladies understand English?' I inquired.

'Nyet!' came the unanimous response.

'Then,' said I, 'I don't mind telling you all that you have lovely ...'

And here, I confess, transported by the air of gaiety which surrounded me, I used a word which had not to my recollection passed my lips since my Army days, and certainly has never since. Sensing, perhaps, its meaning from my glances, the little charmers giggled with delight and, seizing my arms, skipped away with me. As I went I caught a glimpse of Rogozhin ushering Holmes through the wings past a sign bearing an arrow and the words DRESSING ROOMS.

For the following portion of this deplorable narrative (one which it has taken me many years of hesitation to determine to set down) I am indebted – if that is an appropriate word in the circumstances – to Sherlock Holmes. There had been frequent occasions upon which our friendship had almost floundered, but none more so than this. Yet, painful though the events were to me at the time, I conceive it my duty, as biographer and historian, to record without omission all that Holmes told me of his share in them, and my only reservation has been to withhold the facts from the public at large until the appearance of these posthumous papers. Here, then, is the verbatim account of that disgraceful evening, in the words of Sherlock Holmes himself.

Having watched Watson being borne away by that giggling bevy, bestowing his lascivious glances quite indiscriminately amongst them and bearing every resemblance to a satyr of pronounced English origin and antecedents, I allowed myself to be guided by the sinister Rogozhin along a passageway whose squalor was in marked contrast to the tinsel glitter that is the outward countenance of the romantic stage. As we went he leaned towards me and, to the accompaniment of a sickening wave of perfume, murmured confidentially, 'Mr. Holmes, I must prepare you. This is not ordinary case.'

'It is only the extraordinary that interests me,' I assured him. 'Working as I do rather for the love of my art than for any other consideration, I refuse to associate myself with any investigation which does not tend towards the unusual, and even the fantastic.'

'Excellent!' he cried, drawing away to my intense relief. 'No, no, Mr. Holmes, this is not ordinary case. Not extraordinary. Is *extra*-ordinary.'

Rubbing his hands with every appearance of glee, he rapped deferentially at a door bearing a card upon which were written large the words MADAME PETROVA. The door opened and an elderly woman of Slavonic aspect appeared. They exchanged words and the woman, evidently some sort of maid, held the door ajar for us to enter. As I passed her I noticed a gleam of what might have been amusement in her eyes and she quickly put her hand to her mouth, I fancied to stifle a smirk. She stepped outside and closed the door.

The room was small and in elegant contrast to what else I had seen of the backstage regions of this great theatre. Soft drapes, mirrors and cascades of flowers were much in evidence. The lighting was soft, chiefly emanating from two elaborate candelabra upon a dressing-table, at which sat the unmistakable Madame Petrova, still clad in her feathery, jewel-encrusted costume, undoing her hair.

With a bow, Rogozhin spoke some words which I took to be an introduction. Not having had occasion to number Russian amongst the many languages with which I am familiar, I am unable to reproduce the exchanges between the ballerina, who clearly spoke no English, and the director-general, but will content myself with conveying their gist.

Madame Petrova turned on her stool to face me with a beaming smile, extending her arm and hand. I took the long white hand and bestowed on it the kiss which convention demanded. I stepped back and was subjected to a head-to-foot scrutiny by a pair of huge, darkly lustrous eyes. She spoke again.

'Madame says you are shorter than she expected,' Rogozhin interpreted.

'That was not my intention,' I replied, and was about to expound a theory of mine about the relationship between height and the deductive faculties when the ballerina interrupted with a torrent of words.

'Madame says, "Short, tall, who cares? It is the brains that count." '

I regarded her with new-found respect. I am not, as is well known, a whole-hearted admirer of womankind, but I could not listen to her clear-cut flattery without realizing that here was a woman whose path no vain man could cross unscathed. My delight was immediately added to when Rogozhin went on, 'Madame is great admirer of yours. She has read every story. Her favourite is *The Big Dog from Baskerville*.'*

With incredible grace Petrova rose from her stool and, with a backward glance in my direction, passed behind a screen, over the top of which certain items of female attire began one by one to appear. I deduced that she was undressing. A wave of scent told me that Rogozhin was again at my side. He was opening a violin case.

'Mr. Holmes, you know about fiddles. What is your opinion of this one?'

He drew forth an instrument of superb colouring and an elegance of line that caused me to catch my breath involuntarily. Seizing it from him I peered through one of the frets and, as I had expected, was able to read the words "Antonius Stradivarius Cremonensis, Faciebat Anno 1709.' I plucked the string, then turned to Rogozhin.

'The label is authentic. Judging from the shape, the colour of the varnish and the tone, I have no hesitation in saying that this is a genuine Stradivarius of the best period.'

His crafty eyes gleamed.

'You like?'

'It is magnificent.'

Petrova's voice sounded from behind the screen.

'Madame says, "Take it. It is yours." '

'Mine?' I echoed, incredulous.

* Watson again; or is it Holmes this time? *The Hound of the Baskervilles* was not published until 1902, 17 years after this conversation, and not in Russian until many years later.

'For services you will render.'

'My professional charges are upon a fixed scale. I do not vary them, save when I remit them altogether.'

His features working with disappointment, he reached out to take the instrument from me. I held on to it.

'This, however, would seem to be the exceptional occasion.'

He beamed again and once more rubbed his hands. There was a rustle from behind the screen and Madame Petrova emerged, wearing a superb peignoir of brocade with velvet trimmings and, if I was not mistaken, little else. She glided sinuously across to a Recamier chaise longue and arranged herself upon it.

I heard, rather than saw, Rogozhin swallow. He said hoarsely, 'I will pour vodka and explain.'

A frosted silver bucket stood beside the chaise, containing a bottle draped in a napkin. The director-general took up the bottle and poured from it into three glasses. The vodka was pink. He addressed me over his shoulder.

'Mr. Holmes, what you have seen tonight is last and absolutely final performance of Madame Petrova. She is retiring.'

'What a shame,' I said.

'She has been dancing since she was three years old. And since she is now thirty-eight . . .'

'I should not have said she was thirty-eight.'

He turned his head briefly. 'That,' he said with a slight lowering of his voice and one eyelid, 'is because she is forty-six.' He turned again to Petrova and, with a deferential leer, handed her a glass of vodka.

'So,' he continued, turning to me again, 'Madame has decided to leave ballet and spend life bringing up her child.'

'Admirable.'

'Problem now is to find father.'

'He is missing?'

'Correct.'

'And that is why you wish to retain my services?'

'Also correct. We must have father, because without father, how can there be child?'

'I see,' I responded more slowly. 'The whole thing is still in the planning stage.'

'Correct yet again. Madame would like child to be brilliant and beautiful. Since she is beautiful, she now only needs man who is brilliant.'

He turned to Petrova, who was watching us uncomprehendingly, a slight smile on her lips. Evidently sensing that the kernel of the interview had at last been reached, she fixed her large eyes upon mine and held me with a long gaze. She raised her glass, then, with a sudden tilt of her swan-like neck, dashed its entire contents down her throat. A clash of tonsils beside me told me that Rogozhin had done the same. I took a sip and found my throat instantly engulfed in fire, which ran searing along my tongue and sent its fumes swirling into the cavities of my head, making my nose smart and my eyes run.

'What is in this?' I managed to gasp.

'What does it taste like?'

'Red pepper.'

'That is what is in it.'

Rogozhin filled Petrova's glass and his own, then turned to me to interpret her latest remark.

'Madame wish to know how soon you can be ready?'

'Ready?'

'To leave for Venice. All arrangements have been made. You will spend one week there with Madame . . .'

'Well,' I stopped him, 'this is all very flattering. But surely there are other men? Men better equipped . . .?'

'To tell the truth,' he confided, leaning unpleasantly close, 'you were not first choice. We considered our Russian writer, Leo Nikolayevich Tolstoi.'

'A genius.'

'But nearing sixty. Ideally too old. We then considered the philosopher, Nietzsche.'

'A first-rate mind.'

'Too German. Also Piotr Ilyich Tschaikowsky. Alas, it was a disaster.'

'Why?'

'How shall I put it? Women are not his glass of tea.'

'A pity,' I said.

A further torrent of Russian issued from the languid figure upon the chaise. Rogozhin beamed upon me again and might have embraced me, had I not fallen back a judicious step.

'Madame is very happy with her final choice,' he said fervently.

'Madame must not be too hasty. She must remember I am an Englishman.'

He nodded respectfully. 'So?'

'You know what they say about us. If there is one thing more deplorable than our cooking, it is our love-making. We are not exactly the most romantic of people.'

'But that is perfect! We do not want some sentimental idiot who will fall in love and perhaps commit suicide when all is over. Only one week in Venice, and you go back to London with Stradivarius, Madame back to Russia with baby.'

The gist of this must have been apparent even to the ballerina. Nodding vigorously, she cried something which I can only render as *'Ju uzhe vibrala imena – Alexei ili Svetlana.'*

Her meaning was plain to me, even before Rogozhin could interpret: 'Alexei if is a boy, Svetlana if is girl.'

'Svetlana Holmes,' I murmured, more to myself than to them. There was, I had to admit, a certain euphony; an agreeable cadence. Hastily pulling myself together, I said, 'Mr. Rogozhin, as to my medical history, I am afraid I neglected to mention one detail which might be of importance. There is haemophilia in my family. We are all, as the term goes, bleeders.'

He translated rapidly and anxiously, but the smile returned to his lips at her reply.

'Madame says not worry. She will not scratch you.'

'That is reassuring,' I agreed, 'but . . .'

There was, for the first time, a ring of impatience in the veritable Niagara of words which gushed from the ballerina, and a troubled expression upon Rogozhin's countenance as he addressed me again.

'Madame says you talk too much. You find her attractive, or no?'

Before I could answer there was a rap at the door. It opened and the flushed face of a man peered round, to the accompaniment of distant gypsy music. I recognized the features of Watson, distorted as they were by a stupid grin and half-glazed eyes. His hair was tousled and he wore a flower behind one ear.

'Excuse me,' he addressed Rogozhin in slurred tones. 'What does *pro . . . prokaznik* mean?'

'It means "You little . . ." – what do you say? – "rogue".'

Watson beamed tipsily.

'I hoped it did. Thank you.'

His gaze traversed the room, passed me over unnoticed, and came to rest on the peignoired figure on the chaise longue. His bloodshot eyes widened and he stood ogling for some moments. I fancied he was about to step into the room, and, indeed, that may have been his intention; but in attempting to move he swayed backwards, momentarily out of sight, and Rogozhin deftly seized the opportunity to close the door. He turned the key and repeated his question to me.

'Please answer, Mr. Holmes. You find Madame attractive, or no?'

I have always felt of Watson that, if not himself luminous, he is a conductor of that light which burns so brightly and steadily in myself, and his brief appearance on this occasion had given me an idea which would not otherwise have occurred to me until some seconds later. With a smile and a slight bow in Madame Petrova's direction, I answered Rogozhin without further hesitation.

'I find her most attractive – that is, for a woman.'

'Then no problem!'

'Perhaps a slight one.' I endeavoured to simper a little. 'You see, I am not a free man.'

'Not free? But you are bachelor.'

'Precisely. A bachelor who, for the past five years, has ... lived with another bachelor.' I paused fractionally before continuing. 'Five very *happy* years.'

His brows beetled.

'What is this you are trying to tell us?'

By pinching myself surreptitiously in a tender spot I was able to cause a blush to appear in my cheek.

'I had intended ...' I hesitated ... 'hoped, that is, to avoid the subject. There are those of us, Mr. Rogozhin, who, through a cruel caprice of Mother Nature ...'

'Get to point!' he snapped.

'The point is that Tschaikowsky was ... was not an isolated case.'

I lowered my gaze in becoming embarrassment, noticing,

as I did, a slight crusting of vegetable matter along the edges of his shoes which betrayed the fact that he had not arrived at the theatre by cab that evening, but had strolled by way of Covent Garden Market. I heard him growl, in tones of incredulity: 'You mean, you and ... Dr. Watson?'

I nodded, without raising my eyes.

'He is your glass of tea?'

I squared my shoulders and faced him manfully

'If you wish to be picturesque about it.'

There was unmistakable agitation in Petrova's voice as she sought his explanation for the mutual grimness of our expressions. His response brought her leaping to her feet in a swirl of colour. More than once I heard the word 'idiot!' amongst her tirade, and made a mental note to compile a monograph upon words common to the Russian and English languages. With a vicious yet ineffably graceful movement of her arm, she lashed the glass of vodka from her compatriot's hand and sent it splintering against a wall. I seized her hand in its return sweep.

'Madame,' I addressed her, face to face, 'the loss is all mine. But I would rather disappoint you now than in a gondola in Venice.'

I kissed the hand, now tasting powerfully of spilt vodka, and relinquished it. Without waiting for Rogozhin to interpret I turned curtly on my heel, strode to the door and left the room.

So much for Holmes's own contribution to a narrative which, even at this late stage, I am strongly tempted to rend into fragments and commit to the purifying flames. Yet, although I feel the shame burning my cheeks as I write, I feel that to omit one account from this record will be to break faith with my avowed intention, play fast and loose with history, and drive a coach and four through my probity as unbiased chronicler. Therefore, albeit with a reluctant pen, I will continue.

My time during Holmes's absence from my side had not, in a sense, been wasted. Plied by my delightful little friends with alternate glasses of vodka and champagne, I had quickly felt my spirits soar and my senses jig in frenzied time with the accelerating rhythm of the music. I had allowed myself to be dragged forth into the middle of the stage, where, to the accompaniment of cries of encouragement, whistles and rhythmic hand-clapping, I had cavorted step for step with the most bewitching of my entourage. For one wild moment I toyed with the idea of getting down upon my haunches, crossing my arms, and essaying that kicking form of dance which I believe is known as the *gopak* and is much favoured by those members of the Cossack race who have not yet displaced their cartileges; but the remaining vestiges of reason restrained me and I contented myself with endeavouring to lift my winsome partner in that manner which appears so effortless to mere onlookers at a performance of the ballet. Indeed, my efforts met with no small success, and, spurred on by the cries of all, I had raised her above the level of my head when something – it may have been the vodka and champagne – caused me to stagger and my knees to double up beneath me, and we crashed together to the stage, where we lay in a delicious tangle before willing helpers restored us to our feet and pressed replenished glasses into each of my hands.

'Watson!' I heard a familiar tone, high and incisive, above the merry din. 'Watson, are you coming?'

At that instant the orchestra struck up a further melody. I caught my partner's eye. Her feet were already beginning to move, and before I knew what I was about I found myself dancing again.

'Watson!' I heard more sharply at my elbow.

'What is it?' I asked, not missing a step.

'We are going home.'

'Home?' I laughed madly. 'Not a chance. Not the slightest, not the dimmest, not the remotest chance.' I waved airily; and it is with a heavy heart that I dip my pen again and inscribe my final word to him in those surroundings: 'Toodle-oo!'*

As I whirled my partner I saw Holmes's tall figure striding away through the unheeding throng. I also saw Rogozhin appear from the wings, to glance after him with what seemed to be a look of regret and then to scan the scene until his eyes found me. Each time I turned I noticed his eyes still upon me, and even as he crossed to the buffet, seized a glass and drained its contents at a gulp, he continued to stare in my direction with one of the most inscrutable expressions that I have ever seen on human countenance, and on few animal ones.

When I turned back to my prancing partner I found, to my surprise, that she had been replaced by two of her colleagues, and, as I caught a glimpse of the former girl mopping her brow with the hem of her tutu as she made wearily towards the bar, these in turn were cut out by two more. Still my energy seemed unabated. The faster the music played, the more nimbly my feet twinkled, and it was evidently all my partners could do to keep up. I caught a glimpse of the former pair standing with Rogozhin at the buffet, and, the expressions of surprise upon the girls' faces and the glances they constantly darted in my direction, I had no doubt that although he appeared to be doing most of the talking, they had already conveyed to him their incredulity

* It will interest philologists to learn that it was Dr. Watson who coined this expression, hitherto regarded as having originated in, or about, 1905.

that an Englishman no longer in the first flush of youth and without experience should so manage to outstrip in agility lithe and highly-trained professionals. As I whirled again, I found that my latest partners had been replaced by yet another pair, and that the former were now in deep conversation with their sisters, all of whom were now watching me. They had, in fact, been joined by a number of the young men of the company, in whose eyes, as they observed my every manoeuvre, I felt I could read an even more fervent admiration for my prowess.

The balalaikas shrilled as the wild Romany strains rose in pitch and tempo. Hands relinquished mine and clasped again and I felt my partners enjoin me to whirl even faster in that abandoned dance. Turning my head to smile my reassurance that I was equal to their most vigorous demands, I was astonished to discover that my pair of partners were no longer girls, but two smiling youths with flowing, flaxen locks, both wearing short tunics and astonishingly close-fitting tights.

Conceiving this at first to be a supreme tribute to my agility and stamina, I beamed upon them and continued to dance unflaggingly. But to my surprise they were shortly joined by another pair of similarly-clad young men, and then another, until I was dancing only with partners of my own sex, whom the female dancers, now watching keenly from beside Rogozhin at the buffet, made no move to displace.

I felt my step flag and signified by a glance to my companions that I wished to stop. They shook their heads unanimously, and would have spurred me to greater endeavours had I not wrested my hands away from theirs and forced my way from the circle, to march to where Rogozhin stood, an enraptured expression upon his face. The faces of the ballerinas surrounding him were as of stone. Seeing me approach he took up a fresh glass of vodka and proffered it. I made no move to take it.

'What's going on,' I demanded, with some difficulty after my exertions. 'What has happened to the girls?'

He raised his eyebrows.

'Why? Do you not prefer as it is?'

'As what is?'

He smiled strangely.

'You do not have to pretend, Dr. Watson. Mr. Holmes has told us everything.'

'Everything?'

'About you ... and him.'

'About ... !'

'Come now, my friend. There is no need to be bashful. We are not bourgeois. Maybe with doctors and detectives is unusual. But in ballet, is very usual.'

'What is *usual*?'

He gesticulated towards the young men, now dancing contentedly with one another.

'Caprice of Mother Nature. See how happy they are – Pavel and Mischa, Boris and Dmitri, Illya and Sergei ...'

I felt myself stagger, as though from a blow. The room reeled, the mad music shrieked. Images flashed across my eyes – Rogozhin's leering countenance; the dull, cold eyes of the young girls in the abandon of whose smiles I had so recently bathed; the simpering grimaces of the prancing youths.

Without more ado I elbowed and shouldered my way through that demoniac throng, found the street, and employed viciously the tip of my cane to prod into life a dozing cabby, whom I ordered to convey me to Baker Street without mercy to his animal.

Despite the quantity of vodka and champagne I had con-

sumed, I mounted the stairs of 221B two at a time – with the exception, that is, of the seventeenth, which I mounted singly. I burst into our sitting-room, to find the customary haze and reek of tobacco smoke emanating from Holmes's wing chair. I could contain my fury no further than the threshold.

'You wretch, Holmes! Monster! Of all the vile, unspeakable fabrications. I demand an explanation immediately.'

He did not respond. There was only the languid curl of his pipe smoke drifting over the back of his chair. Enraged beyond endurance, I flung my opera-glass case in his direction. It hit the back of the chair with a loud thud, and there came a smaller clatter as Holmes's pipe fell to the ground, with a scatter of glowing ashes.

'Holmes?' I exclaimed, starting forward. 'Are you all right?'

'Perfectly, thank you, Watson,' came his sardonic tone from behind me. Spinning round, I observed him standing in the shadows of a corner of the room. He had replaced his tails with a smoking jacket, and his foot was still poised upon the treadle of his smoking machine. With a cry I leaped to the other side of the wing chair and saw the evidence of the deception which had been practised upon me.

'From the sound of your footsteps, I gathered you were not in a particularly amiable mood,' he said calmly, advancing from the shadows. For the first time in my life I was tempted to assault him.

'How could you do such a dastardly thing to me?' I spluttered. 'What the deuce can you have been thinking of?'

He picked his pipe from the floor and ground out the embers.

'My dear Watson, you have my most abject apologies.

But have you ever found yourself cornered by a madwoman? I could think of no other way of getting out of it without hurting her feelings.'

'*Her* feelings! What about mine? Not to mention my reputation. Have you any conception of the gravity of what you have done? Of the possible repercussions?'

He shrugged dismissively.

'There may be a little gossip in St. Petersburg.'

'I'm not talking about that. I mean *here*. These things spread like wildfire. I can just hear those malicious whispers behind my back. I shall never be able to show my face in polite society again.' A chilling thought struck me. 'If ever this should get back to my old regiment...'

'Pshaw!'

'You don't know the Fifth Northumberland Fusiliers. I should be struck off the rolls. My pension would be finished.'

'Watson, you are in danger of running amok.'

'... Disgraced, dishonoured, ostracized. What am I to do?'

'Might I suggest, for a start...'

'Well?'

'... that you get rid of the flower behind your ear?'

I seized the forgotten bloom, my mind running swiftly and fearfully over my journey through the streets, and dashed it to the ground at Holmes's feet.

'You may think this is funny, Holmes, but let me remind you that we are both in the same boat. We must take desperate measures to stop this talk. Quite clearly, we cannot continue to live under the same roof. We must go our separate ways.'

'Though,' he replied with that irresponsible mockery which he reserved for baiting me to my limits 'we can still see one another clandestinely – on secluded benches in Hyde

Park, perhaps, or in the waiting rooms of suburban railway stations.'

'Rubbish!' I exclaimed, my anger diverted from Holmes himself to that imagined legion of scandalmongers. 'We have nothing whatever to hide.'

'That is what I have been trying to tell you.'

'Let someone start a rumour – let us hear just one word – and we must not hesitate to sue for slander.'

'My dear Watson, no one would dare. Your record with the fair sex is not only enviable but, as a result of your printed boasts, widely known.'

I chuckled modestly.

'I must confess that there are women in three continents who would be prepared to vouch for me. No doubt you, too, could produce evidence that would satisfy any court on your behalf.'

I spoke these words more as a statement than as a question requiring an answer. Nevertheless, I was somewhat surprised that he made no response.

'Can you, Holmes?' I felt obliged to persist.

He turned towards his room.

'Good night, Watson.'

'No, Holmes, wait.' I hurried forward to bar his way. 'I do not wish to pry, and I assure you that the matter would hold no concern for me if it were not for the possibility of legal action against those who might seek to sully our good names. I must beg you to forgive the presumption, and ask you straightforwardly – have there been women in your life?'

For a long moment he stood still, his penetrating gaze searching my face as if seeking something there. At length he spoke.

'The answer, Watson, is yes – I *will* forgive the presumption.'

Gently pushing me aside, he went into his room and closed the door, leaving me to ponder yet more deeply the complex enigma that was Sherlock Holmes.

At our breakfast table the following morning neither alluded to the events of the previous night: I, because the belated effects of the vodka and champagne made articulation difficult; Holmes, for I knew not what reason. He was just cracking the shell of his fifth egg when there came a knock at our door.

'Who can that be at this hour?' I croaked.

'It is Mr. Rogozhin, director-general of the Imperial Russian Ballet,' answered Holmes without so much as a second's pause for thought. 'He is carrying a violin case in his right hand and a bouquet of flowers in his left.'

'How on earth can you know this?'

'Because he has somewhat rudely opened the door without waiting for our bidding and is standing behind your chair.'

I spun round – injudiciously, in view of the state of my head – and found Rogozhin as Holmes had described. His smirk gave his countenance a resemblance to an open tin of syrup.

'Did you say come in?' he asked, advancing towards Holmes.

'I did not.'

'Thank you. Mr. Holmes, you are leaving in such hurry you are forgetting Madame's present.'

He held up the violin case.

'I did not forget it. I did nothing to deserve it.'

Rogozhin grinned repulsively.

'Neither did Tschaikowsky, but Madame gave him grand piano.'

Shaking with mirth that was unlovely to see, he pressed

the case into Holmes's hands. Holmes lifted the lid and I craned forward to glimpse the magnificent instrument which lay within.

'Accept it, Holmes,' I urged, thinking that here might be the very interest which would alleviate the boredom which made him victim to his vile habit. He nodded.

'I am overwhelmed. Kindly convey my thanks to . . .'

Rogozhin leered.

'Madame incommunicado. You will be pleased to hear that she is on her way to Venice where she will join famous French painter. She met him last year in Paris, at Moulin Rouge.' A momentary concern furrowed his brow. 'One can only hope that child will grow up to be normal height.'

Hastily demolishing his egg, Holmes withdrew the violin from its case and began to stride about the room, tuning its strings. Rogozhin turned to me and upon his countenance there appeared the kind of look a politician wears when about to kiss an elector's baby. He held up the flowers.

'Is for you.'

'For me?' I took the bouquet gladly. 'Madame Petrova is too kind.'

He darted a glance at the preoccupied Holmes and leaned towards me, to say in a half-whisper: 'Not from Madame. Meet me at Savoy Grill, eight o'clock tonight.' He grinned sickeningly. 'And not send landlady!'

With a gay cackle and a bow to us both he pranced out of the room. For a moment I remained immobile, my senses paralysed by the enormity of it all. Then the dam burst, the floodgates were torn aside, and the torrent of my fury rushed through. I do not remember what I said, and, if I could, should not repeat it here. I only know that, minutes later, when the tidal wave had receded and the boiling waters subsided, I turned to my companion to see the hawk-like features in repose, eyes closed, mouth set in a slight, unaccustomed smile, as the bow rose and fell and a dreamy, melodious passage from Tschaikowsky issued from the violin whose origins, as my readers will, I am sure, appreciate, I have until now seen fit to disguise from them.

CHAPTER FOUR

THE GIRL FROM THE RIVER

THE time has now come to reveal the most intimate aspect of Sherlock Holmes's life – his one and only involvement with a woman. (I exclude his encounter with Miss Irene Adler, which I have chronicled in my account of *A Scandal in Bohemia*, choosing to reserve the word 'involvement' for other meanings.)

Though I may be accused of sensationalism, I have faced worse risks. As I have already stated in this memoir, the only purpose of these fresh revelations is to prove once and for all that Holmes was by no means only the impersonal thinking machine of which I have perhaps given too strong an impression in my published accounts of his singular career, but a man akin to other men, subject to the same temptations and human failings as the rest of us.

There is no denying, however, that the case which I am about to relate was a sensational one in many ways, including in its ramifications such disparate and even incongruous elements as a diabolical mechanical device, a group of Trappist monks, and even – if the adjectives which I have just employed may be forgiven in this connection – Her Majesty Queen Victoria.

The year was 1888, and the date – unforgettable to me – 17th April. It was evening. All day a thick dun fog had filled Baker Street, veiling the tall houses with yellow vapour, drifting into alley-way and passage as though the spirits of ancient inhabitants sought to return to their dwelling-places.

Traffic was sparse and slow; the plodding hoof-beats of cab-horses, and the gruff cries of their drivers, mingled with the coughing of the few pedestrians unlucky, or rash, enough to be out and about. In vain the street lamps, flickering as though gasping for air, strove to penetrate the dirty yellow murk.

A cheery fire burned in our grate, close to which I sat, in my customary chair, reading the *Evening Standard*. Holmes lay outstretched on the chaise longue, playing his violin, a feat which I have often admired and thought might be adopted to advantage in the concert hall by those virtuosi who distract their audiences by prowling, writhing and jigging as they perform.

Insulated from all mankind by the thick blanket of fog which enshrouded the building and had silenced the rattle and murmur of Baker Street below, we seemed to inhabit a cosy, softly-lit world of our own, whose only sounds were the occasional crackle of the fire, the hiss of the gas, the soulful notes from the Stradivarius, and the rustle of my newspaper as I turned a page.

It was I myself who at length disturbed this peace, throwing down the paper in disgust, unable to suppress a snort of 'Stuff and nonsense!'

'Not at all,' rejoined Holmes, still fiddling. 'Theme and Variations, Corelli.'

'To think,' I continued, 'that a serious newspaper like the *Evening Standard* should waste its columns on such foolishness ... Tchah! Loch Ness Monster, indeed!'

'Really? Has it been sighted again?'

'For the third time this month, according to this. It is variously described as having a long neck, a twenty-foot tail, and a hump on its back.'

'Clearly, a cross between an eel and a camel,' suggested Holmes, embarking upon another variation.

'How, then, would you account for the smoke they say comes out of its nostrils?'

'Oh, I should say that we are dealing with a beast of great passion, that has come up from the depths in search of female companionship.'

I chuckled. 'If you ask me, the whole thing smacks of *delirium tremens*. Someone's been drinking too much Scotch whisky.'

The remark provoked a swift-running train of thought whose terminus was a well-charged decanter on our sideboard. I arose from my chair, flexed my relaxed muscles, and made for the sideboard, pausing en route to draw aside the curtains and peer into the yellow night.

'What a night for a murder,' I remarked. A sudden spasm in my right buttock* caused me to wince and add, 'Or rheumatism.' I was about to turn aside and seek that sovereign cure for all discomforts when the sound – rare enough on that night – of a horse's hooves and cab wheels made me hesitate and peer out once again. Momentarily, the swirling fog parted sufficiently to enable me to see, by the haloed yellow lamplight, a hansom drawing up at our very door. No passenger alighted, but the cabby jumped down, glanced up at our fanlight, appeared to consult something in his hand, then crossed the pavement to our door. As the bell jangled faintly below I turned to Holmes.

'Are you expecting someone?'

'Not at this hour.'

'Perhaps Mrs. Hudson is entertaining.'

'I have never found her so,' replied Holmes, stifling my groan with a deft arpeggio.

My curiosity aroused, I stepped to the door and opened it, to peer down from the head of the stairs. The acrid smell of the fog greeted me. The street door was open and our

* It may have been in my left shoulder. I am writing from memory.

landlady, Mrs. Hudson, in dressing-gown and some form of nightcap, appeared to be arguing with the man outside.

'What is it, Mrs. Hudson?' I called.

She turned to look up at me.

'There's a cabby here says you owe him two-and-six, sir.'

'What for?'

The man stepped forward into the light. He was a youngish fellow, his countenance bearing all the delineations of an East End Londoner.

'What is it, my man?'

'The fare, guv'nor.'

'I owe no fares.'

'The young lady, guv'. She don't have any money.'

'What young lady?'

'Here.'

With this he stepped back out of my sight again, to reappear with the sagging figure of a woman, her fair hair lank and dishevelled, her features deathly pale. She clutched a coarse blanket tightly about her.

I hurried down the stairs. The woman was evidently in her early thirties. Her features, at close quarters, were strikingly handsome, but a fresh bruise disfigured her temple and I was now able to see that her hair was soaking wet. I noted that she wore a wedding ring and that one of her shoes was missing.

'What has happened?' I demanded.

Beautiful but lustreless eyes searched mine briefly, before she answered in a slurred tone, 'I don't know.'

Her foreign accent was apparent even in so brief an utterance. The cabby spoke up.

'That's all she keeps saying – "I don't know".'

I heard Holmes's violin playing cease, as I moved forward to question the man.

'Where did she come from?'

'The river. I was driving down the Embankment, just below Westminster Bridge. I heard a shout. I stopped to look. There she was in the water, drowning.'

'Gracious!' Mrs. Hudson exclaimed.

'It wasn't easy, guv'nor, what with the cold water, and the dark, and her fighting me. . . .'

'Why did you bring her here?'

We all turned to look upward at Holmes, on the landing, violin and bow still in his hand.

'Because I found this in her hand,' the fellow replied, holding up a square of soggy cardboard. '221B Baker Street. That's right, ain't it?'

I examined the card and nodded.

'What did you want at this address?' Holmes asked the girl.

She continued to stare up at him stupidly, as though finding it difficult to focus her vision.

'I . . . don't remember.'

'Well, Holmes?'

The cabby shifted his feet restlessly. 'Well, gentlemen, if you want her, it'll be two and six. Or,' he added with a touch of that loveable Cockney humour shared by omnibus conductors and the like, 'shall I throw her back in the river?'

I let him see my displeasure.

'Mr. Holmes . . .' Mrs. Hudson began imploringly, but there was no need for her to continue.

'You had better accept delivery, Watson,' said Holmes.

Nodding my emphatic agreement, I found a two shilling piece and a sixpence in my pocket.

'Here you are, my man. Keep the change.'

'Thank you, guv',' the merry fellow responded, 'and there'll be no extra charge for the use of my horse blanket.'

So saying, he snatched the blanket from about the girl and was gone into the impenetrable night. Mrs. Hudson hastily shut the door and I moved to the girl, who was clutching her arms about soaked clothing, her form shaking and her teeth chattering.

'You are shivering,' I said, placing one arm around her. I could feel the cold of her body through the thickness of my clothing. 'Come along. Let us get you out of those wet clothes.'

'I'll be up in a moment with some tea,' said Mrs. Hudson, disappearing rapidly into her quarters. Unresisting, the girl accompanied me with dragging footsteps up the stairs and into our warm apartment, where I at once settled her into a fireside chair and commenced to chafe her icy wrists to restore her circulation.

As she lay back, utterly weary, I noticed that her clothing was not only wet through, but dishevelled and torn. The bodice of her dress was rent, revealing a generous glimpse of an enchanting bosom through shreds of what I judged to be expensive lace. She wore an overdress of well-cut corded silk, and around her shoulders lay a knitted woollen shawl, upon which her long, fair hair had escaped from a once-elaborate coiffure, to fall in drenched tendrils. Her eyes alternately closed and opened, to betray restlessness, apprehension, and even, I fancied, fear.

'She is suffering from shock and exposure,' I told Holmes, who had stooped to take from me the damp piece of cardboard bearing our address. He examined it closely.

'Written in soft pencil. There was some printing on the back, in blue, but it has been washed away by the water.'

I turned my attention to the bruise on the girl's temple.

'Look at this, Holmes. She's had a nasty blow.'

'Could she have hit her head when she fell, or jumped, into the river?'

'No. The blood had already coagulated. She was struck deliberately, Holmes. This is possibly a case of attempted murder. Hand me my bag, if you please.'

He did as I requested. As he knelt beside me, the girl opened her eyes again and her bewildered gaze flickered between us.

'Who ... are ... you?' she asked, half-whispering.

'I am Dr. Watson. This is Mr. Sherlock Holmes. Do the names mean anything to you?'

'No.'

'Think.'

'I ... am trying.'

'Can you think of your own name?' Holmes put in.

Her brow furrowed with the effort. She shook her head.

'She has obviously suffered concussion,' I told him. 'It often leads to temporary amnesia.'

I drew from my bag some cotton wool and a bottle of antiseptic, in which I proceeded to soak it. The girl winced as I touched her wound with it, but lay quietly, her eyes closed, as I swabbed gently.

'So, all we know,' Holmes mused, 'is that she was struck on the head, thrown into the Thames, and subsequently cast up into our laps.'

'We know much more than that,' I disagreed. 'Her accent tells us that she is foreign. Her ring – I raised her hand – says she is married.'

He reached down and picked up her remaining shoe, which had slipped from an elegant foot. He showed me inside it the imprint, only slightly worn, BAZAAR MODERNE.

'Are you French?' he asked the girl. *'Vous êtes Francaise?'*

'Non.' She seemed to have to concentrate her mind. *'Je ne suis pas Francaise.'*

'She says she's not French, yet she answers in French, Holmes!'

'*Vous êtes Suisse?*'

He moved behind her chair and gently moved her head to one side, enabling him to turn back the collar of her dress and find the label.

'*La Femme Elegante, Bruxelles,*' he read out. '*Vous êtes Belge? De Bruxelles? Bruxelles!*'

She hesitated a moment longer, then answered haltingly, '*Je pense que . . . oui. Mais je ne suis pas sûr.*'

I heard the rattle of Mrs. Hudson's tea tray behind me as Holmes gently eased the wedding ring from this strange young woman's hand. She made no effort to resist. The ring was of copper. He showed me the inscription inside:

'GABRIELLE – EMILE 5/11/83.'

'Your name is Gabrielle?' Holmes asked her.

She nodded slightly and murmured, 'Gaby . . .'

'Your husband's name is Emile?'

'Emile?' she echoed vaguely.

'Where is he?' persisted Holmes. 'What are you doing in London?'

Mrs. Hudson handed me a steaming cup of tea, which I placed in the girl's hands and motioned her to drink. She sipped tentatively, then gratefully.

'What are you doing in London?' persisted Holmes.

'I do not know.'

'What happened at the river? The river? Think. *Pensez! Concentrez vous!*'

Her face suddenly crumpled and she was racked with sobs.

'Emile . . .!' she cried.

'That's enough, Holmes,' said I. 'I won't let you question her further in this condition.'

With a sigh of defeat he slipped the ring back on to the girl's finger and left my side.

'Mrs. Hudson,' I ordered, 'put her to bed, please. You may use my bed. I shall sleep on the couch.'

'Come, my dear.' murmured our kindly landlady, easing the sobbing girl to her feet and holding her against her own comfortable form, as they went slowly into my room.

'She had better have a sleeping potion,' I said, and proceeded to mix one.

'I think she would be better in hospital, Watson,' said Holmes, picking up his pipe and lighting it, his customary preliminary to deep thought.

'Under no circumstances,' I demurred. 'She shall have all the medical attention she needs from me. More importantly, she must be protected. There has been one attempt upon her life already. There may be others.'

He stared at me thoughtfully for some moments before replying.

'This temporary amnesia – how temporary is it?'

'It depends upon the extent of the injury. It is like a series of veils, shrouding her memory. Like that fog out there. It could clear swiftly or might linger for days.'

'Even weeks?'

'Possibly.'

Holmes paced restlessly.

'Watson, these are not spacious apartments. We don't wish to clutter them up with women.'

'Holmes, we have never had a case such as this. *A* woman comes to us – is brought to us – with a problem of some sort. She had our address and was no doubt intending to consult us before this . . . incident occurred. We don't know who she is, nor what her problem may be. Isn't that the kind of challenge you're always praying will come your way?'

'I quite agree. But we can't afford to wait for those veils to lift from her memory. We must break through them as quickly as possible.'

I regarded him anxiously.
'You feel it is so urgent?'
'I do.'
He crossed to the window, parted the curtains and stood puffing at his pipe, looking out into the swirling night out of which our visitor had so dramatically come. I picked up the teacup in which I had mixed the sedative and went with it into my room.

CHAPTER FIVE

GABRIELLE

My experience of camp life in Afghanistan had at least had the effect of making me a ready sleeper in most circumstances, and despite the discomforts of our couch I soon fell off – to sleep, that is – and was at once plunged into an agreeable dream of the day when I received a letter from Her Majesty's Government advising me that my wound pension had been quadrupled, whereupon I placed a whole month's accumulation upon a 100–1 outsider in the Derby, won hands down, and was invited by the animal's beautiful, young and titled lady owner to return with her to her moated castle, where, behind raised drawbridge, I spent halcyon hours in a recital of my reminiscences, interspersed with amorous dalliance.

In consequence of these preoccupations, I remained unaware of any nocturnal activity in our more humble Baker Street abode. Learning on the morrow of what had transpired, I requested Sherlock Holmes to give me his account, for inclusion in my notes, and I append it herewith.

Watson, having administered his sedative to our enigmatic young guest, curled himself upon the couch beneath a blanket and was shortly snoring away in his customary disgusting fashion, twitching strangely from time to time as though in the grip of some nightmarish dream from which he would have been glad to be released. I contemplated wakening him, but decided that, since a certain amount of suffering is good for the soul, I would let him be.

Mrs. Hudson had retired to her bed and, with the exception of Watson's garglings and gobblings, all was silent in the house and outside. Even unseen, the presence of the fog could be sensed eerily, and I was glad to seek the comfort of a chair beside the glowing fire in my bedroom, where, watched only by the portraits of notorious criminals which adorned my walls, I sat, smoking my pipe and pondering, oblivious to time or the need for sleep.

My mind, during those long hours, ranged over many possibilities suggested by the young woman's fragmentary story, and again and again I found myself re-examining that small square of cardboard with our address on one side and the smudge of blue ink on the other. Yet I could find no explanation for her evident intention to consult me, and even less for the murderous assault which, but for a quirk of fate, would have prevented her from ever reaching Baker Street.

It was with a start, and a mouth like burnt shoeleather, that I suddenly realized that the light of dawn was filtering beneath the window blinds, and that I had consumed the best part of half a pound of the strongest shag tobacco. But the repetition of a small sound told me that it was not the dawn light that had disturbed my reverie. It was a small voice outside my door; and even as I heard it again there came the click of the doorknob and the creak of the opening door.

'Emile?' I heard the voice of our visitor. 'Is that you, Emile?'

I had risen to my feet, and now stepped quickly into a patch of shadow beyond the dying firelight's gleam as she came into the room. She was what I can only describe as naked.

'Yes, Gabrielle. It is I,' I responded, thankful that she had chosen English as her means of communication with her imagined husband.

She moved swiftly to where I stood.

'Ah, Emile! I thought I would never find you.'

She flung her arms about me.

'Hold me. Hold me tight.'

I held her tight, and do not think it necessary to elaborate upon those four words.

'It's been such a long time,' she was murmuring in my ear. 'You know what I did before I left Brussels?'

'What, Gabrielle?'

'You won't be angry with me, Emile? I bought myself an expensive negligée. Come with me.'

'A negligée?'

'A pink negligée, with maribou feathers.'

She released me suddenly and moved towards my bed, adding, 'Don't you think that's foolish for a married woman?'

'Where ... where is the negligée?' I heard myself say in a voice I barely recognized as my own.

'In my luggage. Come here.'

I slowly approached the bed.

'Where ... is ... your luggage?'

She extended her arms towards me.

'I don't know. Come, my love.'

I was just hesitating whether to obey or to shout for Watson when I noticed something on the palm of one of her beckoning hands. Taking the hand, I contrived swiftly to examine it. In the same blue ink as the smudge on the cardboard square were what appeared to be the letters I, O and a Greek E. Ignoring her supplications, I reached across to my washstand and picked up my patent magnifying shaving mirror. Holding it to the palm of her hand, I was able to read distinctly the reverse image – the number 301.

Beyond this point in his narrative I was unable to persuade Holmes to proceed. Remarking somewhat strangely, 'You are so much better at that sort of thing than I, Watson,' he insisted that I take up my account once more from the point where, in excruciating pain, I awoke that morning to find myself, with initial surprise on our sitting-room couch with daylight streaming through the windows and Mrs. Hudson conveying steaming plates from the dumbwaiter to an already-laid breakfast table. I groaned.

'Hadn't you better get up, sir?' she demanded without hint of sympathy. 'Your porridge will get lumpy.'

I groaned again.

'I should ... like to very much,' I responded, turning with difficulty upon my stomach. 'Mrs. Hudson, would you mind placing your knee in the small of my back.'

'I would mind very much,' she bridled. 'The very idea!'

'Please, Mrs. Hudson. I'm ... in ... very great ... pain.'

I heard her approach, somewhat hesitantly, and a moment later felt the tentative thrust of a knee against my back.

'A bit higher,' I instructed. 'Just below the seventh vertebra.'

I felt her obey.

'That's good. Now, put your arms under mine and fold them behind my neck ... Now, give it a good snap.'

She jerked mildly.

'No, no. Show no mercy. Bear down on me ... Ah!'

There came a sudden wrench and a distinct snapping sound.

'That's better!' I exclaimed, disengaging myself to sit up and rub my neck. 'That confounded couch.'

I was making for the table when the reason for my having been on the couch, and the events of the night before, came flooding back into my mind.

'Great heavens! Our patient.'

Mrs. Hudson smoothed her dress.

'You start your breakfast before it spoils, Dr. Watson. I'll see how she is.'

I sat down and she crossed to the door of my room; but I had barely dipped my spoon when I heard her cry from within, 'Dr. Watson! She's gone.'

In an instant I was with her in my doorway, looking past her towards my empty, disordered bed. I turned to Holmes's closed door.

'Holmes!' I cried. 'Holmes! She's gone.'

I flung open Holmes's door and was advancing to take the motionless form by the shoulder when I saw something which made me freeze in my tracks.

'Mrs. Hudson!' I called automatically.

She hastened to join me, and side by side we gazed down upon the sleeping form of the young woman. A single blanket covered her, and, on the evidence of what remained visible of her body, she was unclothed.

'Well, I never!' I heard Mrs. Hudson's scandalized cry.

Recovering from the shock, I was just about to point out to her that although the woman lay in Holmes's bed, Holmes was not beside her, nor anywhere else in the room, when we heard the sitting-room door open and Holmes's briskest voice cry, 'Mmm! Porridge, I fancy; though lumpy again, no doubt.'

We found him dressed in Inverness and deerstalker and carrying a large suitcase bound with leather straps, under one of which was tucked a white parasol. He set the suitcase down on the couch and I was able to observe a tag hanging from it bearing the figures 301 in blue.

'There you are, Holmes,' I cried as casually as I was able, allowing my glance to flick significantly towards his bedroom door. 'We were just wondering...'

'We certainly were,' Mrs. Hudson agreed, in a tone which I had heard her use on a number of occasions when threatening us with eviction as a consequence of Holmes's chemical experiments or indoor revolver practice.

He commenced removing his hat and coat.

'Mrs. Hudson,' said he, obviously unperturbed, 'why don't you go down to the kitchen, get a towel, and wipe that look of disapproval off your face?'

'Holmes...!' I intervened, but our landlady was already marching, head high, to the door, which she slammed behind her.

'You can't really blame her, Holmes. I mean to say... Dash it, if I didn't know you better, even I might suspect you'd taken advantage of the young woman.'

'As a matter of fact,' said Holmes, stooping to examine the suitcase, 'I did take advantage of her. May I ask you to pass me the butter knife?'

I was half-way to the table before the import of his words struck me.

'You did *what*?'

'The butter knife, if you please, Watson.'

I took it to him. He commenced to work with it upon the suitcase locks. His nonchalance infuriated me.

'Holmes, this is totally reprehensible. A woman in distress – under our protection.... Where are your professional ethics? Have you no sense of decency, of shame?'

'None whatsoever. If you must know, I found her body quite rewarding.'

'*Holmes!*'

'Especially the palm of her right hand.'

My mind reeled.

'For heaven's sake, spare me at least the details.'

'Oh, very well. Then I need not bother you with the particulars of how I traced her suitcase.'

My innate curiosity overcoming anger, I said more mildly, 'That is her suitcase?'

'Certainly. You recall that piece of soggy cardboard with our address on it? It was a luggage ticket. The number had rubbed off on the palm of her hand. And since she would be most likely to have arrived from Brussels by the boat train, I concluded that her baggage would be deposited at Victoria Station.'

'By Jove! If you're right we should find the clue to her identity.'

The last of the locks gave way under his probing knife. He rapidly undid the straps.

'At least we should find a pink negligée...'

'A pink...?'

'With maribou feathers,' he cried triumphantly, lifting the garment out and letting it fall from its folds. 'Voila!'

'What else is there?' I wondered, beginning to search. After some moments combing through a delightful froth of clothing I was rewarded with a tied bundle of letters and a framed photograph of a quite handsome man of about fifty years of age. Holmes took the letters from me and was about to loosen the binding when some instinct caused him to turn sharply.

'Come in, Madame Valladon,' he cried.

I, too, turned, in time to see our guest, clad in Holmes's dressing-gown and walking unsteadily, come to a surprised halt, staring at Holmes.

'You *are* Gabrielle Valladon?'

'Yes.'

Her widened eyes fell upon the open suitcase.

'I apologize for ransacking your case. But since you came to us for help...'

She steadied herself against a chair back.

'Where am I?'

'At number 221B Baker Street.'

'Oh... yes.'

Her gaze traversed us both.

'Which of you is Mr. Holmes and which is Dr. Watson?'

Holmes smiled.

'Watson is the handsome one.'

I could not forbear to tug modestly at the ends of my moustache.

'At least, that is the way he affects most women. Allow me.'

He helped her into a chair. I hastened to the breakfast table and poured a cup of coffee, which she took thankfully and sipped for a moment, before saying, 'My head is full of cobwebs. It is all so confusing.'

Holmes seated himself opposite her and pressed the tips of his fingers together.

'Then let us try to sort it out. You came to England looking for your husband?'

She appeared surprised at his knowledge, but answered readily enough.

'Yes. He is a mining engineer. We were married five years ago, in the Congo.'

'Where your husband was working in a copper mine.'

'Yes. But how did you know that?'

'Your unusual wedding ring – it is made of copper.'

'I see!'

'And now you are having to search for him,' prompted Holmes. She nodded, the troubled expression returning to her eyes.

'Last year he invented a new kind of air pump. He was engaged by an English company.'

'Its name?'

'Jonah, Limited. He came here to work, while I have lived in Brussels until we should decide upon a permanent home. We have been writing to each other regularly. Then suddenly, three weeks ago, his letters stopped. I kept writing, expecting ... But there came no answer. Finally, I decided to go to that address.'

She gestured towards the bundle of letters still in Holmes's hand. Over his shoulder I read on the back of one of the envelopes '32 Ashdown Street'.

'And did you?'

'Yes. It was just as empty shop. No one was there at all. Then I have tried to find Jonah, Limited.'

Her voice trembled.

'No such company exists.'

'Madame Valladon,' Holmes asked seriously, 'can you think of any reason why your husband should have lied to you about these things?'

'Emile lie? Never. He loves me. I love him.'

Holmes nodded. I found it necessary to clear my throat. Bravely controlling her emotions, she went on.

'I went to the police. They said they would send out a report that my husband was missing, but that they could not be too ... too encouraging. Then I went to the Belgian Embassy and explained the situation to them. It was they who suggested I consult you, Mr. Holmes.'

'The best advice they could have given,' said I.

She nodded. 'I was on my way here, when ...'

She passed a hand across her brow.

'It is so difficult to ... There were suddenly footsteps behind me. I had no reason to be afraid, but then at once came a hand over my mouth and the smell of chloroform.

The next thing I knew, I was in the water, drowning . . . and then a man was wrapping me in a blanket. . . .'

'A passing cabby,' I told her. 'By some miracle he saw you and was able to rescue you and bring you here.'

'Madame Valladon,' Holmes urged her, 'someone tried to kill you last night. Have you any idea at all who that might have been?'

She shook her head.

'I do not understand any of it.'

Her voice rose.

'Mr Holmes, what does it mean? Where is my husband? You must help me find him.'

I patted her shoulder.

'We'll do our best, be sure of that.'

Holmes had risen and crossed to his desk. He returned, bearing paper, pen, ink and an envelope. He placed them in her hands.

'I wish you to write one more letter to your husband.'

I handed her a blotter upon which to rest the paper and held the ink well for her. She dipped the pen and wrote on the envelope, to Holmes's dictation:

Emile Valladon,
32 Ashdown Street,
London, N.W.

'But, Mr. Holmes, I tell you, there is nobody there. It is . . .'

'Pray do as I say.'

She finished the address and he took the envelope from her. She dipped the pen again and waited with it poised for the dictation to resume, but, to both our surprise, Holmes merely took the blank sheet of paper, folded it and inserted it in the envelope, which he sealed.

'You are sending a blank sheet of paper to an empty shop, Holmes?' was my puzzled question.

'The empty shop, my dear Watson, is obviously being used as an accommodation address, or, at least, somewhere at which letters will be delivered and may be retrieved. The question is *how* are they collected, and by *whom* – but most of all, *why*?'

So saying, he motioned me to assist our puzzled young friend to the breakfast table, touched the bell for Mrs. Hudson, ordered eggs and rashers for all three and a plentiful further supply of hot coffee, and, as she was about to leave, handed her his strange missive, with instructions to see it into the post without delay.

CHAPTER SIX

THE DUCCHESS

AT the time of which I write, the central area of London enjoyed a dozen postal deliveries a day, a service which was subsequently scandalously diminished to ten. Even in the outer districts the postman's tread and cheery whistle could be heard at all times of the day; and it was clear, therefore, that we should have no time to lose in pursuing Holmes's plan, outlined over breakfast, that we should reach Ashdown Street before the envelope, in order to observe what, if anything, became of it after its delivery to the empty shop. Accordingly, as soon as the meal was ended Holmes, Madame Valladon and I took a cab round Regent's Park and through the mean and often sordid streets of Camden Town, paying it off a little farther along in the direction of Highgate and continuing our journey on foot.

Our object was to approach our destination as inconspicuously as possible, but I could not help feeling that a trio comprising the striking figure of Holmes, in deerstalker and cape, the beautiful Madame Valladon, in her stylish Continental clothes and large, be-feathered hat, and myself, in morning coat and bowler, must have looked somewhat out of place afoot in those shabby streets. My opinion was evidently borne out by the youthful denizens of the neighbourhood, who followed us in small packs, jostling, hooting and mimicking Madame Valladon's delightful feminine gait and my own limp. Holmes ignored them, striding purposefully towards our goal, and after aiming a number of kicks at those nearest to me and treating them to a few expletives, delivered from the side of my mouth lest Madame Valladon should hear and understand them, I followed his example and affected not to notice our tormentors, who, finding themselves deprived of the chief satisfaction of their sport, which was to goad their victims into violent reaction, grew less and less noisy and active, and at length, to a final fusilade of catcalls and gestures, fell away behind us.

The streets which we now entered unmolested were narrower and quieter, with fewer passers-by and tradesmen's vehicles. Several properties, I observed, stood empty and dilapidated, as though despairing of ever being tenanted again. No. 32 Ashdown Street proved to be one such, a dirty, seemingly abandoned corner shop with the bottom half of its windows obscured by paint.

Holmes cautioned us to walk briskly past the property, seeming to pay no heed to it. Immediately round the corner was the narrow entry to a noisome yard, into which he led us. Grimy, eyeless walls rose up on every side, but I heard Holmes's hiss of satisfaction at the sight of a barred window in that wall which could only be the side of No. 32. We peered together into a dusty, littered interior of empty, cobweb-hung counter and shelves and the melancholy air of a place that has seen life pass for ever. A closed door was in the rear wall of the shop, evidently giving access to a street or area behind. On the floor, close to the door, stood a large, square object, covered with a tarpaulin sheet.

Holmes tested the window bars with both hands. The masonry in which they were embedded was corroded and flaky and there was distinct movement to the grille. Holmes grunted and, to Madame Valladon's evident astonishment, proceeded to unscrew his walking cane into several separate sections, housing respectively a chisel, straight hammer and metal saw.

'Why not the shop door?' I suggested. 'It will be locked, but you could pick it easily enough while we keep guard.'

'I observed as we passed that it has a heavy padlock,' Holmes answered, beginning to work on the base of the grille. 'It would take some time and we must not be observed.'

'The back door, then,' I persisted, pointing to where our alley turned sharply off to what must have been the rear of the block of shops.

Holmes shook his head.

'Where there is one back door, there may be others, and windows. Not all these buildings are untenanted, and one might well harbour someone with more than a casual interest in callers at No. 32. No, Watson. Here we may work unseen, but I shall be obliged if you will take a cautious peep round that corner and back into the street from time to time.'

I did as he instructed. The alley gave on to a mews at the back of the shop, and, as Holmes had surmised, several windows overlooked it, some of them bearing evidence that the buildings were occupied. Some children were playing, but I remained unseen and returned to Holmes. He had made excellent progress and within a few minutes more had chipped away enough of the setting of the metal bars to enable him to swing the grille inward, as on a hinge. He climbed on to the sill and disappeared into the shop, returning in a moment to the opening to motion us to follow. I assisted Madame Valladon and climbed in after her. Holmes proceeded to reassemble his cane, and used it to push the grille back into place.

As I glanced round that dingy interior, with the dust of ages thick upon every surface, I was surprised to hear what seemed to be the twittering of many small birds, such as one is aware of in the aviaries at the Zoo. It seemed to emanate from the far side of the room. I followed the sound and paused before the tarpaulin-covered object near the inner door. I pulled back a corner of the heavy sheet. The box-shaped object it covered was a large cage, in which perched and fluttered dozens of brightly coloured canaries.

'Holmes ...!' I began, but he swiftly motioned me to silence with a finger against his lips and a glance towards the front door of the shop. The letter-box was opening, and an envelope fell through, to lie on the dusty floor. I moved towards it.

'No, Watson,' Holmes ordered, in a low voice. 'Leave it there. Our object is to see what happens to it next.'

I pointed to the floor where the letter lay.

'Look, Holmes. In the dust – tracks of wheels. Someone has been here recently with some sort of trolley.'

He nodded. 'You will note also that they run from this front door to that door in the rear and back again.'

'What can it all mean?' asked Madame Valladon, her pretty face puzzled. 'What must we do?'

'I am afraid,' answered Holmes, 'that what faces us now is the most nerve-racking part of the detective's calling – doing nothing. We must just wait and see what happens next.'

I looked about for some form of seat to offer Madame Valladon, but there was nothing that, even if suitable, would have been fit to come into contact with her clothes. There was nothing for it but to stand there, waiting and hoping.

'Mr. Holmes,' said Madame Valladon at length, 'I do not know how I am going to pay you for your help. All the money I had is in my purse, somewhere at the bottom of the Thames.'

He smiled.

'It could be worse than that. You could be at the bottom

of the Thames, much to your discomfort and my chagrin.'

She returned his smile, and I noticed that, for a moment, their eyes held each other's. I cleared my throat.

'What I don't see, Holmes, is how anybody picks up letters here.' I pointed to the dust. 'I mean to say, no footprints. Just these tracks. What do you suppose it means?'

'If it were not for a conspicuous absence of ice, I should deduce that someone was entering and leaving the room upon skates.'

He crossed to the birdcage.

'Or perhaps these are not canaries after all. They're carrier pigeons, picking up the letters as they arrive and . . .'

He broke off abruptly and returned to Madame Valladon. Her eyes had filled with tears.

'Forgive me,' said Holmes. 'I should not have been flippant. I know how worried you are, and . . .'

Once again he was compelled to halt in mid-sentence, this time holding up his hand for silence to both of us. Over the fluttering and chirping of the birds I distinctly heard a more rhythmical squeaking sound. It seemed to be behind the closed rear door, and approaching. After a moment it ceased, and there came the rattle of a chain being unfastened. I looked round swiftly for some place of concealment, but saw none. Holmes beckoned to us to follow his example and flatten ourselves against the rear wall of the shop in such a way that the opening door would hide us from view.

There was the grate of a key turning, and the door squeaked open.

As the squeaking resumed, I realized at once what it was that had imprinted those tracks in the dust. There came into sight not a trolley, but a wheelchair of vintage design, its spoked wheels protesting shrilly at every turn at the lack of oil and attention that had been bestowed upon them. Seated in the chair and propelling its wheels with gnarled and withered hands was an old woman, unfashionably dressed and with her white hair straggling about her. In her lap I could see a bulky paper bag and a tin vessel which seemed to contain water.

She wheeled herself straight to where the covered birdcage stood, and with surprising strength threw off the tarpaulin and cast it over a beam joining two upright posts which ran from floor to ceiling close to where we stood rigidly waiting to be discovered. Fortunately, her eyes were only for the occupants of the cage.

'Good morning, my pretties,' she greeted them, to the accompaniment of an excited outcry and a great deal of flying and fluttering against the bars.

'Here's Mum with your breakfast. Did you think she'd forgotten you, then?'

She unfastened a catch and opened the cage door, to pour grain from her paper bag into a small feeding trough. From the jug she poured water into another, beset by the birds which danced around her hand.

'Now, now! No pushing. There's enough for everybody. Some of you will be going on a little trip soon, and you'll need your strength for that. Mum will hate to lose you, but even an old woman has to live. Although,' she added with a bitter edge to her voice as she closed the cage door, 'you might well ask why.'

Seeing the birds feeding happily, she glanced round the room, though fortunately in every direction except towards where we stood. Her roving glance fell upon the envelope inside the front door and she propelled herself briskly enough to where it lay, picked it up and studied the address closely, but made no move to open the envelope.

My ear registered the sound of horses' hooves and wheels in the mews outside the back door. The old woman heard it a moment later and her head jerked round. Dropping the envelope in her lap, she swung her wheelchair round and made directly towards our place of concealment. I tautened my muscles, ready to follow Holmes's lead – but once more we were undetected, due to the cover of the door and partly, I fancy, because the woman's attention was upon the two men who strode heavily into the room.

'Morning, Duchess,' one of them greeted jovially, still out of my sight, to which the other added, 'What you been doing with yourself, then?'

'What do you think?' the old woman responded, in the same jocular vein. 'Taking dancing lessons.'

The two men stepped into my sight. From their aprons and leggings I took them to be carters. The elder one carried a small birdcage, with which he made towards the bigger cage.

'How many do you want this time?' the woman asked, wheeling herself to her cage and fumbling with the catch again.

The man placed the small cage on the floor not more than a few feet from our hiding place and helped her with the door. I could see that its bottom was covered with newspaper.

'Two dozen,' he replied. He picked up the small cage and held it close to the other, while the woman transferred the wildly flapping little birds.

'Three ... four ...' she counted. 'What are they doing with all those canaries, anyway? What's going on up there?'

The other carter answered. 'Look, Duchess, we don't know and we don't want to know, see?'

'... seven ... eight ... I only asked.'

The man with the cage grunted. 'When you work for Jonah, it's better not to ask anything.'

'... ten ... eleven ... that's one dozen. One ... two. ... Who's Jonah, anyway?'

'Keep counting, Duchess.'

She tossed her head contemptuously. '... three ... four ...'

A bird suddenly struggled from her grasp and began flying wildly about the room.

'Shut that door!' ordered the man with the cage to his mate. The other man turned and came across to the door, which he jerked shut with a bang.

I gave silent thanks that the old woman had got well into the second dozen before a bird escaped her. A minute earlier, and the closing of the door would have revealed the three of us pressed against the wall. As it was, at a gesture from Holmes, we had already crept behind the tarpaulin draped across the beam and were continuing our observation from there.

Halfway to freedom, the canary did not propose to surrender easily. Both men were soon pursuing it from perch to perch, and I felt sure that at any moment it must fly in our direction and lead them to us. However, it landed on the sill of the window through which we had climbed and there fatally hesitated. The older man crept towards it and seized it in one enormous hand. As he did so, he knocked against the loosened grille, which promptly collapsed and fell from the frame.

Once again I feared that the moment of suspicion leading to discovery had come. But the man only grinned as he stuffed the bird into the small cage.

'You better get some new bars put in, Duchess.'

'Oh, yes? And a boiler and a water closet while I'm about it?'

The birds were now safely transferred and both cages secured

'Two dozen it is,' said the old woman.
The younger man indicated the envelope in her lap.
'That to go too?'
'No. That's going to be picked up in person, that is.'
She gave a little cackling chuckle, which made the two men glance at one another and grin. The older man picked up the small cage and stumped towards the door.
'Bye, Duchess. And get your wheels oiled.'
He jerked the door open wide and his mate followed him out. The old woman grimaced after them and squeaked her way across to a shelf, where she placed the envelope. Then she returned to her cage and the remaining birds.
'Sleep well, my pretties. Mum'll see you tomorrow.'
Her hand reached out for the tarpaulin and whisked it down. Her face registered no astonishment at seeing us there – for she did not see us there. Anticipating the sequence of her actions, Holmes had already led us once more behind the open door.
She draped the sheet over the cage, glanced finally round the room, then, taking her jug and paper bag into her lap again, propelled herself out of the back door, which she pulled to behind her as she passed through. We heard the rasp of the lock and the rattle of the chain once more, and then a final receding squeak as she wheeled herself away.
I lifted my hat and mopped my streaming brow.
'I thought our goose was cooked that time,' I admitted, and I could read in Madame Valladon's face a clear account of the strain she, too, must have felt. Holmes, needless to say, was his usual casual self.
'The art of concealment, my dear Watson, is merely a matter of being in the right place at the right time.'
'Mr. Holmes, did you hear what she told them?' Madame Valladon asked anxiously. 'The letter is to be collected in

person. Do you really think, then, that my Emile is going to come here himself for it?'

'It would certainly simplify matters if he would,' Holmes answered.

'Holmes,' I said, 'what was all that about Jonah? And that talk of "up there". Where d'you suppose *is* "up there"?'

'My guess would be Scotland. To be more precise, Inverness.'

'What on earth makes you say that?'

'Didn't you notice the newspaper in the bottom of the smaller birdcage.'

'As a matter of fact, I did.'

'Did you notice *what* newspaper it was?'

'Well, no.'

'How often have I said to you ...? But let it pass. It was the *Inverness Courier.*'

I was about to rejoin that the presence of the *Inverness Courier* in the bottom of a birdcage was hardly conclusive evidence, when I was forestalled by a cry from Madame Valladon. She had wandered across to the shelf where the letter lay and had picked it up. Holmes cried out when he saw it in her hand.

'No, no! It must remain exactly where it was placed.'

'But it is not the letter.'

'Not ...?'

She held it out.

'It is addressed to you.'

'That's impossible!' I exclaimed, stepping forward to examine it. 'We sent it ourselves.'

Holmes took the envelope and studied it.

'Nevertheless ...'

With a sudden movement he ripped it open. A single sheet of notepaper lay inside; but I could see as he unfolded it that it was not our paper, and that there was writing on it. A slow smile spread across Holmes's face as he read the note.

'Listen to this, Watson. On the notepaper of the Diogenes Club.

My Dear Sherlock,

I expect you and Dr. Watson to join me at the Club immediately upon receipt of this note. According to my calculations, that should be at 11.40 a.m.

Your Brother,
Mycroft.'

My hand had gone automatically to the chain upon which my late brother's watch hung. I snapped open the case.

'Well?' said Holmes.

'11.43.'

'Then, my dear Watson, either your watch is wrong or Mycroft has miscalculated. And, knowing Mycroft, I suggest you re-set your watch. Come along, Madame Valladon. I fancy we may be able to hail a cab at the end of this road.'

CHAPTER SEVEN

MR. MYCROFT HOLMES

IN *The Greek Interpreter*, one of my narratives for the *Strand Magazine*, I have recorded my surprise upon first hearing Sherlock Holmes mention the existence of his brother Mycroft. It will be recalled that this occurred at a time when our association was already of some years' standing, during which I had never heard Holmes refer to any living relative and had come to the conclusion that he was an orphan. Then, one evening, he had mentioned in casual conversation that he possessed a brother, a man of remarkable talents in the field of crime detection whose inherent laziness and lack of ambition alone prevented him from becoming the greatest criminal agent that had ever lived.

'Again and again,' Holmes had told me, 'I have taken a problem to him and have received an explanation which has afterwards proved to be the correct one. And yet he was absolutely incapable of working out the practical points which must be gone into before a case could be laid before a judge or jury.'

'It is not his profession, then?' I had asked.

'By no means. What is to me a means of livelihood is to him the merest hobby of a dilettante. He has an extraordinary faculty for figures, and audits the books in some of the Government departments. Mycroft lodges in Pall Mall, and he walks round the corner into Whitehall every morning and back every evening. From year's end to year's end he takes no other exercise, and is seen nowhere else, except only in the Diogenes Club, which is just opposite his rooms.'

I suppose I must anticipate that by the time this present narrative is made public the face of London will have been altered through the inexorable demands of 'progress', financial greed, misguided attempts to impose new upon old, and even – though I pray it may not be so – by the consequences of warfare. Much that is venerable will, of course, remain, and many ancient institutions continue to flourish. Whitehall and the Mall will, I feel sure, still exist in one form or another: whether the Diogenes Club will is another matter. In case it does not or if it does is unknown to my future readers, I hope I may be forgiven for devoting a few lines to describing that remarkable institution; to which purpose I feel I can do no better than quote Sherlock Holmes's explanation to me as we walked to the Club, where he had invited me to meet his brother that first time, just before the incident of the Greek interpreter came to our notice.

'There are many men in London, you know,' he had told me, 'who, some from shyness, some from misanthropy, have no wish for the company of their fellows. Yet they are not averse to comfortable chairs and latest periodicals. It is for the convenience of these that the Diogenes Club was started, and it now contains the most unsociable and unclubbable men in town. No member is permitted to take the least notice of any other one. Save in the Strangers' Room, no talking is, under any circumstances, permitted, and three offences, if brought to the notice of the committee, render the talker liable to expulsion. My brother was one of the founders, and I have myself found it a very soothing atmosphere.'

These words now returned to my mind as we again approached Pall Mall from the St. James's end, having returned Madame Valladon to our Baker Street abode and the secure charge of Mrs. Hudson. I had not met Mycroft Holmes again, nor set foot in the Diogenes Club, since the conclusion of the Greek Interpreter affair. He had, if I had interpreted him properly at the time, hinted that he would be prepared to put forward my name for membership, but I had affected not to understand. Being of a decidedly gregarious nature, there was no attraction for me in the idea of belonging to a club whose dignified dining-room contained only individual tables, each with its single chair, whose homely card room was equipped only for the playing of Patience, and whose magnificently vast billiard room accommodated fully a dozen tables, at each of which I had glimpsed a solitary player, competing in silence with himself.

We ascended the steps of the imposing Palladian-style edifice and were confronted by the reception desk, a veritable barricade manned by an old warrior whose beribboned chest spoke of livelier and noisier campaigns than that which he now waged.

'Gentlemen?' he inquired in a whisper. Any form of greeting would doubtless have run counter to the principles of the Club.

'To see Mr. Mycroft Holmes,' replied my friend, his strident tone for once subdued.

'Yes, sir. He is expecting you in the Strangers' Room. If you will both sign the register – surname, Christian name, address, nature of business...'

He had turned aside to open a huge leather-bound register. I felt my companion pluck at my arm. He jerked his head slightly and I followed him through the swinging, glass-panelled doors which led to the reading-room, a backward glance showing me the defeated campaigner raging silently.

The reading-room was high domed and cavernous, its serried array of statuary giving it a resemblance to a marble quarry in which a horde of sculptors had been turned loose to work *in situ*. As motionless as the statues themselves, a dozen or so men were slumped deep in leather armchairs, occupied with newspapers, books, sleep, or, for all anyone might have noticed, death. Not a newspaper was lowered, not a head turned as we crossed the wide floor, our footfalls muffled by the deep carpeting. The only sound was the slow ticking of a grandfather clock.

As we neared the far door, Holmes paused beside the chair of an ancient member who had fallen into heavy slumber, his *Times* in his lap, a still-burning cigar between his fingers. Holmes picked up an ashtray and held it beneath the cigar, just in time to catch several inches of ash as they broke off. He scrutinized the ash closely, and sniffed it, before replacing the ashtray and ushering me through the door.

'Jamaican, without a doubt,' he murmured in the deserted passage. 'But whether Tropical or Golosina ... no, I really can't quite say.'

Shaking his head with annoyance, he pushed open a fine, tall door and preceded me into the Strangers' Room, the scene of my first meeting with his brother. I well remembered the elegance of these surroundings – towering shelves of volumes in fine leather bindings, antique terrestrial and celestial gloves, gleaming, polished tables upon which rested scientific instruments of glittering brass, marble busts of English statesmen, and, in pride of place, Her Majesty Queen Victoria.

At first I thought that Mycroft Holmes was not, after all, in the room, whose only occupant was busily engaged at a long table, turning the handle of a little cradle, in which lay a bottle of wine. As he cranked, the bottle tilted, delicately pouring its contents into three large glasses without the least disturbance to the sediment.

His delicate task completed, he turned.

'Ah, Sherlock! Dr. Watson. Come in, come in.'

I was astonished by the change in him. Readers of my account of the Greek Interpreter case will doubtless recall my description of Mycroft Holmes as 'absolutely corpulent'; and in a subsequent account – that of the case of the Bruce-Partington Plans, in which we were again associated with him – I remember so far forgetting decorum as to term him 'gross' and to see in his appearance a suggestion of 'uncouth physical inertia', albeit redeemed by the masterful brow, alert glance and other evidences of a penetrating and dominant mind.

The man who faced us on this occasion, impeccably frock-coated, was imperially erect and, if not lean, comparatively slim, and brisk in his movements. He sported a silken cravat, with a pearl pin, a monocle and a military moustache.

I noticed the slight rise in my friend's eyebrows.

'You are looking remarkably fit, Mycroft. How is your gout?'

'Under control. You are evidently well, too, Sherlock. And,' turning to me, 'you also, Dr. Watson.'

'Thank you.'

'What an admirably thrifty woman that Mrs. Hudson of yours must be, Doctor. A treasure.'

'How so?'

'I observe that halfway through cleaning your left boot this morning she finished the contents of one tin of polish and began a new one. The transition from the stale to the fresh is clearly apparent. A less careful servant would have started with the new tin, throwing the last contents of the old to waste.'

He picked up two of the glasses of wine and proffered them to us.

'I have a treat for you – a very old Madeira, 1814 to be precise. There are only six bottles left in the world. I have two of them and am negotiating for a third.'

'If I may say so, Mr. Holmes,' said I, 'anyone who is susceptible to gout should not be . . .'

'My dear Doctor,' he held up a hand: 'the last member of your profession who warned me about that was crossing Piccadilly when he slipped on some orange peel and was run over by a delivery van from Fortnum & Mason. Your very good health.'

We drank.

'Delicious!' I declared.

My friend nodded agreement, holding his glass to the light to study the wine.

'Why are you wasting this precious bottle on us, Mycroft?'

'Wasting? My dear Sherlock, I see you so rarely. How long has it been. Not since the case of the Greek Interpreter. Has anything more been heard of those two rascals?'

'Nothing. Nor of Sophie Kratides.'

'Hm! Something will before long, mark my words.'

'Then I may yet add a footnote to my account,' I said.

'Depend upon it,' said Mycroft Holmes. 'It would be unlike such a girl to let such wrongs against her brother and herself go unavenged. I rather fancy there will be some enigmatic report of a stabbing, in some foreign place, in circumstances suggesting that the two Englishmen had quarrelled and inflicted mortal injuries upon each other. Yes, something of that sort, I fancy. Prague, perhaps? Or Budapest.'

I sipped the wine again.

'Superb! How old did you say this is?'

He regarded me over the rim of his own glass.

'1814. One year before Waterloo.'

'Remarkable!'

'Have you ever visited the field of Waterloo, Doctor?'

'Never. In Belgium, isn't it?'

'Quite.'

Mycroft Holmes turned to his brother.

'Speaking of Belgium, Sherlock, it has come to my attention that you are interested in the whereabouts of a certain engineer.'

I could almost hear the cerebral thunder and see the lightning fork as the brothers stood face to face and strove to pentrate each other's minds.

'I am.'

'I see.'

Another sip of the wine. Then:

'I can save you a lot of trouble.'

'I should be grateful for any suggestion.'

'I have only one – that you pursue the matter no further.'

'Have you a particular reason for saying so?'

'Because the national security is involved. We are handling this matter ourselves.'

'We?' I could not restrain myself from asking.

'The Diogenes Club, of course,' replied my friend, never taking his eyes from his brother's.

'I didn't say that,' returned Mycroft sharply.

'Nevertheless, I see it is true. I have always suspected some underground connection between this dull and seemingly calcified establishment and the Foreign Office.'

'That is neither here nor there. Many of our members . . .'

'It seems to me,' Sherlock Holmes continued, 'that the Diogenes Club is here, there and everywhere. When there are rumblings of revolt in the Sudan, an expedition subsidized by your club conveniently arrives to study the source of the Nile. If there is trouble along the Indian frontier, what happens? A party of your fellow members appears in the Himalayas, allegedly looking for the Abominable Snowman.'

The door opened at this moment and a young man in morning clothes approached Mycroft Holmes, handed him an opened telegram, and, without a word, withdrew a pace or two.

'What a fertile imagination my young brother has,' said Mycroft to me, smiling. 'At the age of five, by carefully observing a neighbour's house, he was able to deduce that babies were not brought by the stork, but by the midwife, in her satchel. Yes, Wiggins? What is it?'

'An immediate answer is requested,' responded the young man.

Mycroft Holmes examined the telegram and paced thoughtfully for a moment before replying.

'Tell them that the three boxes go to Glennahurich, and the red runner goes to the castle.'

'Very good, sir.'

The young man bowed and withdrew. Mycroft Holmes was about to toss the telegram on to the table when he caught his brother's interested gaze. Deliberately, he placed it face downward.

'Why don't you crumple it up and swallow it, to make sure?' my friend suggested.

'My dear Sherlock, there are certain affairs which do not come within the province of the private detective. They have to be dealt with on an altogether different level.'

'In other words, Mycroft, you wish me to stay within my limits?'

'I do indeed.'

'I see. Speaking of limits, what exactly is Jonah *Limited*?'

I detected a subtle change in Mycroft Holmes's expression.

'Sherlock, when I said you should drop this case, it was not merely a suggestion. It was an order.'

'Oh? By whose authority?'

'By the authority of Her Majesty's Government. I *hope* I make myself clear?'

'Perfectly.'

'Very well.'

Our host beamed again.

'Now, if you will excuse me, gentlemen . . .?'

Holmes picked up his hat and I followed suit.

'Good-bye, Mycroft.'

We moved towards the door.

'Just a moment, Sherlock,' his brother called after us.

'What is it?'

Mycroft Holmes tossed my friend his cane, which he had left lying on the table.

'You forgot your tools. Good-day.'

'Holmes,' said I, as we traversed Regent Circus, in the course of our walk back to Baker Street.

'Mm?' was my friend's response, continuing to whirl his cane, to the danger of the public at large, and resuming his irritating whistling of *Loch Lomond*, a tune which he seemed to have got on the brain since our visit to the Diogenes Club.

'Holmes, you will be gentle with her.'

'Eh? Gentle? With whom?'

'Madame Valladon – when you tell her you're giving up her case.'

Holmes made no reply, merely whistled his way to the

end of that banal chorus about 'You'll tak' the high road, and I'll tak' the low road,' or however it is the confounded thing runs.

'Watson,' he asked abruptly, 'what does the word Glennahurich suggest to you?'

'Absolutely nothing.'

'It is a Scottish name.'

'Indeed?'

'And, like all Scottish names, it is really a picture in words. *Glen* means valley; *na* means of the; and *Hurich*, if memory serves me, means a yew tree.'

'I didn't know you had the Gaelic, Holmes. I think you're just making it up.'

When he spoke again it was more to himself than to me.

'So the three boxes go to the Valley of the Yew Tree. Mm!'

'Holmes,' I persisted, 'You *are* dropping the case, aren't you?'

He would not answer, but began whistling again, and I was compelled to keep my own company until we reached 221B Baker Street. After we had ascertained from Mrs. Hudson that nothing untoward had occurred and that her charge was quite safe, and were mounting our staircase, I applied to Holmes again.

'You didn't answer my question, Holmes. Are you planning to disobey your brother's orders? He's not only your brother, remember. You would be defying Her Majesty's Government.'

To my chagrin, he still turned a deaf ear; yet as soon as we were inside our apartments, and Madame Valladon had greeted us and asked if there were any news, he answered, 'Let us just say that I know what our next step will be.'

She regarded him anxiously.

'Yes?'

'I want you to pack your things.'

'Where are we going?'

'At 7.30 this evening, Dr. Watson and I are going to take you to Victoria Station and put you on the boat train.'

I felt a surge of relief within me, but the girl's lip trembled.

'The boat train? You are sending me back to Brussels? Is that it?'

Again Holmes took refuge in silence. He had taken down the current Bradshaw and was consulting timetables.

'Madame Valladon,' I began to explain as gently as I could, 'you must understand that . . .'

She turned from me and stood before Holmes, her cheeks flushed.

'I came here to find my husband. You were going to help me – you, the great detective! Well, perhaps this case is too small for your trouble, but . . .'

I began to explain that, on the contrary, it was being investigated at a higher level than ours, but she had no ears for me. Tears were in her eyes as she continued.

'I won't go back to Brussels. Maybe you're giving up, but I am not. I am going to go on looking for Emile, with or without you. And nobody is going to stop me – even if they try to kill me.'

Holmes closed the Bradshaw with a snap.

'Are you quite finished?'

She was about to begin another tirade, but only a sob escaped.

'If you recall,' Holmes said calmly, 'what I said was that we are going to put you on the boat train. I didn't say that you were going to stay on it.'

'She's not, Holmes? Then. . . .'

'At 7.30 Mr. Holmes and Dr. Watson will be seen waving good-bye to Madame Valladon at Victoria Station. At eight o'clock Mr. and Mrs. Ashdown, accompanied by their valet, John, will appear at Euston Station and board the Highland Express for Inverness.'

'Mr. and Mrs. . . . ?'

I stopped, realizing who Mr. and Mrs. Ashdown were going to be, and, moreover, more than suspecting who was going to fill the role of their valet.

Her tears ended as quickly as they had begun, Madame Valladon stepped forward and kissed Holmes on the cheek. He did not recoil, I was gratified to see: merely murmured, 'That's not necessary.'

With a smile, she hurried away towards my room.

'Perhaps,' said I, when she was out of earshot, 'I should be doing her packing. I'm the valet, after all.'

Holmes ignored my sarcasm and replaced the timetable on the shelf.

'Holmes, exactly what are you up to?'

'As you like to put it in your chronicles, Watson, the game is afoot.'

'No doubt. But what game? Are you really so interested in this Belgian engineer?'

Again he did not answer, and I was stung into more direct rudeness.

'Or is it the *wife* of the Belgian engineer who intrigues you so much?'

All the response I received was the closing of his bedroom door in my face. I turned away, with an impatient exclamation, to find the young woman herself regarding me from my own doorway.

'You don't like me much, do you?' she pouted, moving across the sitting-room towards the couch.

'Nothing of the sort,' I retorted. 'Quite the opposite, in fact. But there is more to this matter than meets the eye. . . . What are you looking for?'

She had picked up her parasol from under the window and was standing there flexing it open and shut, while peering about her.

'My glove. One is here. I cannot see the other.'

I saw it at once, under the couch.

'Here you are.'

She folded the parasol finally and, as she took the glove, gave me the kind of smile that made my hand go instinctively to the ends of my moustache.

'You do not mind helping me?'

I glanced at Holmes's door.

'Not in the least,' said I. 'Madame Valladon . . .'

But she was gone swiftly to my room, and I was left alone to gaze at two closed doors.

CHAPTER EIGHT

THREE BOXES TO GLENNAHURICH

Our train sped northward through the night, past sleeping houses, fields and gardens bathed in moonlight. The outskirts of London were past, the open country of the South Midlands lay about us. Holmes and Madame Valladon had retired to their sleeping-car, while I remained pacing the corridor, gazing at the flying landscape and accustoming myself to the unusual costume concealed beneath my greatcoat. On Holmes, with his astonishing flair for disguise, the garb of a valet would have sat easily: had he not wooed and won a housemaid in the character of a rising young plumber, in the course of one of our adventures? But to me the striped waistcoat I wore gave me a sensation as strange as the knowledge that my friend, firm bachelor and declared misogynist that he was, shared at this moment a sleeping compartment with a young woman of striking attractions.

However lightly he may confess to more serious crimes, it is not easy for a man to admit that he has eavesdropped. For the sake of posterity, however, I must conceal nothing. A burning curiosity drew me moth-like to the door of that compartment. As I bent with my ear to the panel, a ticket-collector startled me by his sudden approach. and straightening myself guiltily I assumed a casual attitude until he was past, then, once again, bent to listen.

A faint rustling, as of garments being discarded, met my ears. Holmes, or Madame Valladon? – and, whichever the disrober might be, what was the other party doing? Imagination boggled, until I heard my friend's usual calm tones.

'You may look now,' he said.

'Thank you,' replied the charming voice of his companion. 'So this is the *robe de nuit* – the chemise – you Englishmen wear.'

'We usually call it a nightshirt,' replied Holmes.

'It is very severe, very classical. Tell me, do you often find yourself in situations like this, Mr. Holmes – in the course of your detective work, I should say?'

I thought I detected a quiver of mirth in Madame Valladon's voice.

'Well, let me see,' answered my friend. 'I once spent a night with a hundred and twenty-one concubines in a rather poorly ventilated seraglio in Constantinople ...'

Fascinated by the promise of the situation, I moved closer to the door and inadvertently fell against it. That was my undoing. Before I could retreat it was wrenched open, to reveal Holmes, in nightshirt and slippers, regarding me quizzically.

'Yes, John? You knocked?'

Stammering and blushing, I replied that I had merely wanted to know whether there was anything Holmes required.

'Nothing,' said he; 'and the name. I would remind you, is Ashdown.'

'Of course, of course. And how is ... Mrs. Ashdown?' I ventured to inquire, craning my neck to obtain a closer view of the compartment's other occupant. Madame Valladon was in the lower berth, her golden hair loose on her shoulders. She wore a deliciously frothy yet concealing garment, and appeared completely at home in this most unconventional situation. I reflected that Emile, wherever he might be, was a lucky man, and that Holmes at this moment, whether he appreciated it or not, an even luckier; and from his normal and unflurried demeanour I feared that appreciate it he did not, although it seemed to me that I detected the very faintest flush upon his usually pale cheeks. In the hope of prolonging the interview, I addressed Madame Valladon.

'Would *you* like anything, er, Mrs. Ashdown? Some mineral water, an extra pillow . . .?'

To my annoyance, the ticket collector again passed me. Holmes called the man back.

'Conductor, if you will examine this man's ticket I think you will find that he belongs in the third class.'

'Is that so, sir? Now, then, you . . .'

He laid a rough hand on my arm. I shook it off, muttering impatiently, 'All right, all right,' threw Holmes a glance in which reproach and anger were equally blended, and started off in the direction of my own compartment. Behind me I heard Holmes's bland good night, and assurance that he would see me in the morning. Then, firmly, he shut the door.

The third class carriage to which my role had condemned me was uncomfortably full of the usual miscellany of passengers: yawning adults and sleeping of fretful children. As I resumed my seat, however, I observed with interest that it also contained seven monks, wearing the habits of their Order and sandals upon their stockingless feet. It must have given considerable pain to one of them, a tall man with piercing eyes and lantern jaw, when I inadvertently stepped on his foot when passing him. To my apology, however, he returned no acknowledgment, continuing to read the sacred book which was absorbing his attention.

I settled myself in the seat opposite to him, and resumed my hat, into which I had coiled my stethoscope in case of possible emergencies during our adventure. A long night lay ahead of us, and I felt it might be profitably spent in conversation with a type of traveller not often met with in England. I addressed the monk genially.

'Going to Scotland?'

He gave no sign of having heard me. I continued my overture.

'I am a valet. My master and mistress and I are on our way to Inverness. You know it, I expect? Beautiful country, beautiful!'

The monk at last raised his head from his book, and, pointing to his lips, shook his head reprovingly. His meaning was clear to me at once.

'Oh, forgive me,' I cried. 'I see that you belong to an Order with a vow of silence. Trappists, are you not?'

Not unnaturally, this produced no reply. Sighing, I turned to look out of the window, but the moon had retreated behind clouds and only blackness met my eyes. I wished that I had brought some entertaining reading-matter with me. The monk, I now saw, was reading the Bible, and the volume was open at the Book of Jonah. I leant across to him once again.

'You're reading the Book of Jonah,' I remarked. 'Curious – only this morning we were discussing Jonah. . . .'

This information did not appear to excite the monk in any way, and I gave up all attempts at conversation.

'Never mind,' I said, and, leaning back in my seat, composed myself to slumber, though not before I had spent some minutes in speculation on the events that were taking place in Holmes's sleeping compartment. No doubt my reader, too, shares something of this curiosity, which I feel it my duty to allay. It is only fitting that what occurred should be told in my friend's own words, as he narrated it to me – many years later – his amazing memory retaining every syllable.

As you know, Watson (Holmes told me), I have the faculty of sleeping at will in any circumstances: I believe Julius Caesar and Napoleon, to name only two great men, shared it. I was not, therefore, disturbed by the fact that while I lay in darkness in the upper berth of our compartment, Madame Valladon continued to read. The berths had thoughtfully been provided with individual gas-lamps, for the benefit of those to whom sleep comes with difficulty.

Lost in meditation, I was recalled from the edge of slumber by her voice.

'Women are never to be trusted entirely – not the best of them,' was her astonishing remark. Surprised, I leaned over the edge of my berth to look down at her.

'*What* did you say? I inquired, wondering if I had heard right.

'I didn't say it – you did, according to Dr. Watson,' she replied, and waved at me the familiar cover of the *Strand Magazine*. 'He gave me some back issues of these,' she added.

I permitted myself a smile.

'The good doctor is constantly putting words into my mouth.'

'Then you deny it?'

'Not at all. I am not a whole-hearted admirer of womankind.'

'I'm not very fond of them myself,' she said thoughtfully, and, gazing at her remarkable beauty and the cat-like grace of her attitude, I reflected that her dislike must certainly be reciprocated by the rest of her sex, who in general prefer to select their friends from those considerably plainer than themselves. I brought the conversation back to myself, for a strange, unwonted urge was upon me to reveal to this enchanting woman facts which I had never before confided to anyone – even the faithful Watson. Her ease of manner, and freedom from that embarrassing coyness which would have characterized almost any other female of my acquaintance in such a situation, impelled me to a frankness I could not have imagined before I encountered Gabrielle Valladon.

'It was St. Bartholomew's Hospital,' I told her, 'that I acquired my mistrust of women, and the somewhat harsh philosophy of which Dr. Watson has so often written.'

'At St. Bartholomew's! Indeed! I didn't know that was a part of medical training.'

'No, no, this was extra-curricular.' She looked up at me with a winning, confiding expression, settling herself more comfortably on her pillows in order to listen.

'It was in my final year as a student of chemistry. I had a young woman assistant.'

'Ah! She was your . . .?'

'No, no. Strong emotion of an amorous kind has always been, as you know . . .'

'. . . opposed to that true, cold reason which you place above all things,' she interrupted again. 'Yes, the good doctor has said this.'

'She displayed an affection for me, which, I must confess, I found somewhat flattering. At length I discovered the real reason for it, and for the long hours she contrived to spend alone with me in the laboratory . . .'

'I can imagine . . .'

'I fear not. It was in order to acquire, without having to sign her name in a chemist's register for it, sufficient cyanide with which to poison her husband.'

'How terrible!' exclaimed my listener.

'Terrible indeed. It was a shock to my nervous system such as I had never felt in my life before.'

I smiled bitterly. 'It was a very small price to pay for a very valuable lesson. Emotional involvement . . .'

'Warps the judgment and clouds the reason, as Doctor Watson has written. That would, of course, explain all the bad poetry in the world.'

'Not that I am against sentiment,' I hastily added, for at that moment I was strangely biased towards it. 'But for one in my profession, it would be fatal.'

'I see,' she replied absently, turning the pages of the *Strand Magazines* scattered on her coverlet. 'What was the title of that story about Constantinople, and the hundred and twenty-one concubines?'

'I fear that issue was confiscated. The publishers paid a substantial fine, and Dr. Watson was put on parole, in my custody.' I glanced at my watch.

'Good heavens! – After one o'clock. Good night, Madame.'

She looked up at me with an inscrutable expression. 'Since we are travelling as a married pair, should it not be at least "Mrs. Ashdown"?'

'Then, good night, Mrs. Ashdown,' I said, smiling.

'Or might it not even be "Gabrielle"?'

'Gabrielle,' I repeated, dwelling on the name with a tenderness I had not heard in my own voice since my student days. It would have been but the work of a moment to descend from my berth to hers, and – but I see my reminiscences are distracting you from the main course of the events you are recording, Watson. Pray continue your narrative.

When we alighted from the train at Inverness Station the following morning I searched keenly the countenances of both Holmes and Madame Valladon, but read nothing in either. As I have recorded elsewhere, he had, when he so willed it, the utter immobility of countenance of a Red

Indian, and the only smoke signals which rose into that clear air were those emitted by his early morning pipe, telling nothing either of satisfaction or remorse. The expression of our fair companion I found equally inscrutable, and when I tested her with a sly wink she either did not – or pretended not to – notice it and turned away to the porter who was unloading our luggage on to a trolley.

'Are all the pieces accounted for, John?' demanded Holmes sharply, and, remembering my role, I hastened to count them.

'All, sir,' said I.

Madame Valladon indicated her parasol, which had been thrust under the straps of her bag.

'I'll take that.'

I removed the parasol and handed it to her, and, as I had seen her do in our apartment, she stood flexing it open and shut in some sort of nervous gesture which, for a moment, sent my curiosity back to the events of her night with Holmes. It was he who broke across my thoughts, addressing the porter.

'How does one get to Glennahurich from here?'

'Glennahurich?' repeated the man in a crusty Scottish accent which made the name sound altogether different. 'Oh, aye. Aboot a mile frae toon. Whyfor d'ye want tae goo thair?'

'The . . . the view,' I answered him, as one working man to another. 'A hill with a yew tree. My master and mistress are partial to picnicking.'

He nodded dourly.

'Oh, aye. It's got a view, all right. But I'm thinking it's no place for a picnic.'

'Why not?'

'Because it's a cemetery.'

He lifted the handles of the barrow and trundled it away.

As we followed him I raised my eyes to the iron footbridge which spanned the rails. Crossing it in single file were the cowled figures of the Trappist monks, and I wondered how, if they were ever so inclined, a Trappist picnic party would conduct its affairs.

Glennahurich proved, indeed, to be a valley, reached by a winding path. The tree which formed part of its name had at some stage multiplied considerably, for there were yews in abundance, with beneath them, leaning and weathered headstones of ancient graves, long forgotten and untended. The long grass stirred about our feet, and a slight graveyard breeze moaned funereally as we wandered amongst the stones, each of which Holmes scrutinized keenly, as though hopeful of finding some connection between this forlorn place and the vanished husband of the young woman who toyed with her parasol at our side.

A movement caught my eye. To my surprise, I saw, advancing along one of the avenues between the rows of graves, a funeral procession consisting solely of men in the formal garb of professional pall-bearers. They carried three coffins, one of normal size and two smaller. A surpliced minister walked behind them, a prayer book open in his hands.

'Two of those must be children's coffins,' murmured our companion, with feminine compassion. 'How sad.'

'Very sad,' responded Holmes. 'No flowers, no mourners. Very sad – and rather odd.'

My heart gave a great leap of excitement.

'Holmes!' I exclaimed. 'Your brother's instructions, remember. "The three boxes go to Glennahurich." '

He nodded composedly.

'I should think you have it, Watson.'

Without approaching too near we moved with the little procession to a part of the cemetery where we observed dark mounds of newly-turned earth, beside which two roughly clad gravediggers leaned upon their shovels. They removed their caps as the cortege approached and stood respectfully while the minister mumbled the words of committal.

It was all ended quite quickly and the coffins lowered reverently into the three new graves. Led this time by the minister, his book now closed, the pallbearers moved away in a ragged group, not bothering to glance in our direction. No sooner had they departed than the gravediggers returned to work, the elder shovelling soil into the largest of the three graves, his colleague working upon one of the two smaller.

Holmes led us to the lip of the large grave. The man looked up, spade poised as our shadows fell across him.

'Good morning,' Holmes greeted him.

The man merely nodded.

'Are they working you hard, Dad?'

The man stuck his spade into the earth and rested.

'Not really.' I found his accent more intelligible than the railway porter's. 'This is healthy country. Sometimes you sit around for weeks on end with nothing to do. Then,' he gesticulated about him, 'you get three in one day.'

'What happened to them?'

'An accident. Father and two sons, they say. They were found floating in the loch.'

'Local people?'

'No. Nobody in these parts knows them. The story goes, their boat capsized in a swell. Ask me, I don't believe it.'

'What do you believe?'

'Well, you can think me an old fool or an old drunkard and I've been called both in my days, and *been* both, I expect – but I've lived around Loch Ness all my life, and when two bairns are pulled out of the water wearing faces like old men from their fear, I say it wasn't just capsizing caused it.'

'You said you were told it was a father and two sons,' I intervened. 'How do you know what they looked like?'

'MacLarnin saw 'em. What he tells me I'll believe any day.'

'Then, if their boat didn't capsize, what did happen?'

The man hesitated.

'What's the use saying?' he said at length, picking up his spade. 'You'd not want to believe.'

'You're not suggesting . . . not this monster we hear of.'

He regarded me for a long moment, and I heard the chink of coins in Holmes's hand. The gravedigger pocketed them and nodded his thanks.

'All I'll say is if you want to take a holiday in these parts, keep away from Loch Ness.'

Both Holmes and I endeavoured to question him further, but he merely shook his head and plied his spade. His mate had completed one of the smaller graves and was already working upon the other, and it was not long before their work was done. Thrusting temporary wooden crosses into the heads of the graves, they shouldered their spades, touched their caps to us, and were gone down the pathway leading to the main road.

'Of all the poppycock!' I snorted. 'Here we are, living in the nineteenth century, and people can still go about believing in nonsense like that.'

'At any rate,' said Madame Valladon, 'although I am ashamed to admit it, it was a relief to hear that they were a father and two boys. It means this could not possibly have anything to do with Emile.'

'It would appear not,' Holmes agreed.

'Then the fact that three boxes were brought to Glennahurich was pure coincidence,' said I. 'But what three boxes are to come here? And who is the red runner that must go to the castle? And *what* castle?'

We were by now moving along the pathway taken by the gravediggers, whom we could see below, wending their way down the road. Suddenly, I felt Holmes's hand on my arm. Without a word he drew me and our companion swiftly aside from the path and into the shade of a yew tree. Climbing up from the road I saw four small boys, in knickerbockers and caps. I was unable to make out their features as they passed our place of concealment, but I could see that each carried a small posy of flowers, and a moment later a lump came into my throat as I watched them go to kneel, two on each side, at the graves of the drowned children. They bent their heads in prayer.

Despite the emotion which charged my voice, I was able to say to Holmes: 'The man said the family had not been identified – that they were strangers in these parts. Then who are these boys bringing flowers?'

'One may feel sympathy even for strangers,' Madame Valladon murmured, clearly affected by the scene. 'It is most touching.'

'They are here,' said Holmes, in his most matter of fact tone, 'because it is their brothers whom we have just seen buried.'

'Their brothers? But how . . .?'

'And they are not boys. Look carefully at their faces.'

He picked up a pebble and tossed it so that it fell with a clatter against a tombstone near to the praying group. Four heads jerked up as one, and for an instant four startled faces were turned so that we could see them clearly. Despite their slight bodies, the boys had the features of mature men.

'Great heavens!' said I.

Holmes nodded. 'They are as tall as they will ever grow.'

'They are . . . how do you say it in English . . . *nains*?'

'Midgets,' I translated for our companion, then turned to Holmes. 'I still don't see...'

'No, Watson? Would it help if I told you they were acrobats.'

'Not at all,' said I.

'Do you remember a tumbling act of six brothers, missing from a circus?'

'Six...? Wait a moment. Yes! The case you turned down. The Six...'

'Piccolos. Some of us,' he explained to our companion, 'are cursed with memories like flypaper. Stuck there is a staggering amount of miscellaneous information, mostly useless, yet by no means always so. See!'

The four midgets had arisen from their knees, replaced their caps and were moving towards where we stood. They passed without noticing us, and this time we were able clearly to see the marks of age imprinted on their features, contrasting so strangely with their boyish stature. They passed and went up towards the road. Led by a pensive Holmes, we returned to stand beside the largest of the three graves. It was Madame Valladon who spoke the thoughts of all of us.

'Mr. Holmes, if those are not children, and it is not children who are buried in those two small graves, then...'

'Quite,' Holmes replied grimly. 'The question is, who lies in this third grave.'

We found out that same night, in circumstances which remain forever imprinted upon my mind. There was no moon and the same dismal wind was whining about us as we left our hotel in the town and trudged once more into that lonely valley. The light of bullseye lanterns led us to the graves. As Madame Valladon directed the lantern beams, Holmes and I thrust spades into the moist, soft earth which filled the largest grave. Our task was easy and within half an hour we had exposed the lid of the coffin which lay there. A few more sweeps of our spades and we were able to lay them aside, and I climbed from the grave to hand Holmes a crowbar. Watched apprehensively by the two of us, his long shadow in that yellow light falling grotesquely across the coffin lid, he worked for a matter of not more than moments before a slight rending sound and a louder snap told us that his work was accomplished.

Standing back so that the full beam of the lanterns was upon the coffin he lifted the lid. I had just time to register its contents – the body of a middle-aged man, arms folded across his chest and on one finger a copper wedding ring – when I heard a cry and a moan from the girl at my side and was just able to catch her slumped form and prevent it from toppling into the grave.

I laid her gently upon the ground, and commenced to massage her wrists.

'Emile Valladon, Holmes?' I asked.

He did not answer, but reached from the pit and took up one of the lanterns, which he shone closely into the coffin.

'Watson.'

'Yes, Holmes?'

'Look at this.'

My gaze followed the beam of the lantern. Neatly laid out upon the satin lining at Valladon's feet were six dead canaries, their once-bright plumage bleached to a grey-white colour.

My eyes caught Holmes's, but neither of us spoke. I returned to my task, and heard the gentle thud of the coffin lid being replaced and the rattle of earth being heaped upon it for the second time that day.

CHAPTER NINE

THE MONSTER

Despite the enormity of the shock she had suffered, Madame Valladon was able, with our assistance, to walk back to our hotel, where I administered a strong sleeping draught. There was no sign of her or of Holmes in the dining-room at breakfast-time on the next day, and when he did appear I fully expected his first words to be that our expedition was ended and that we should go back to London at once and make immediate arrangements for Madame Valladon's return to her native soil. Therefore, I was both surprised and full of admiration to find her following him into the drawing-room, where I sat with the newspaper, and to hear both assuring me that there was to be no question of retreat. Pale yet composed, she insisted that, having found her husband at last, she would not rest until she had discovered the cause of his death, and the reason for it.

So it was that, later in the morning, we set out by carriage along the shore of Loch Ness, that remarkable inland sea which in places is well over one hundred fathoms deep, Holmes and Madame Valladon enjoying the comfort of the passenger accommodation, while I, the less privileged valet, sat beside the driver on his draughty perch.

Fortunately, we were well supplied with rugs, for the cold mists had not yet vanished. Looking down through the trees, we could see nothing of the loch for the cloud of white vapour drifting across it. We spoke little, each meditating on the wild and romantic surroundings in which we found ourselves, so far from humdrum Baker Street. To me the Highlands were an old stamping-ground, for I had done some shooting in my youth. Holmes, too, had visited them before, but I could see that Madame Valladon was awed by the scenery into a temporary forgetfulness of the tragic discovery we had made at Glennahurich.

Our coachman broke the silence. 'Yon's the hotel,' he told us, pointing his whip in the direction of a building glimpsed through the trees round a curve of the road. It was, indeed, the Caledonian Hotel, a plain but pleasant hostelry where we were given a warm Highland welcome by the kilted manager and shown at once to the second-floor room which was to be occupied by 'Mr. and Mrs. Ashdown'. Handsomely and imposingly furnished (though I observed Madame Valladon regarding with some distaste the mounted stags' heads whose glass eyes glared down from the walls in a manner not calculated to soothe the nerves of the visitor), it commanded a fine vista across to the loch, although the water was not yet visible through the mists.

'You'll have a lovely view of it when the mist rolls away,' the manager told us. 'And if you want to do any sight-seeing, here's a wee guide that'll help you. If you're interested in history, now, you'll find you're in Prince Charlie's country. Up yonder, back beyond Inverness, you can see Culloden Moor where the English beat him in '46 – that's a sad spot, indeed. Over the loch, hard by Fort Augustus, there's Glen Moriston, where he hid with the Seven Men from Butcher Cumberland's bloody redcoats ... Begging your pardon, madam.'

A good deal less civilly, the manager showed me to my own small attic room, reached by a narrow flight of dingy stairs. I unpacked hastily and then returned to 'Mr. and Mrs. Ashdown's' comfortable apartment, eager to hear what Holmes might have had in mind for our next move. I was distressed, though hardly surprised, to find the poor young woman sobbing quietly, seated on the edge of one of the beds, while Holmes paced the carpet, keenly examining some small object in his hand.

'Ah, Watson,' said he. 'What do you make of this?'

He handed me a copper wedding ring. A glance at Madame Valladon's hand told me that it was not hers.

'Holmes!' I whispered aghast. 'You don't mean to say you took this from ... from the ...'

He nodded.

'And as I have just been pointing out to our admirably brave and charming friend here, there is a distinct difference between it and her own.'

Averting her face, Madame Valladon held out her ringed hand for me to examine. Bending close and holding her husband's ring against hers, I could see that the copper of which hers was made was quite unblemished, while the other bore a distinct greenish tinge.

'What does it mean, Holmes?'

'It means, as I rather expected, that the cause of Emile Valladon's death was most probably not drowning.'

This unfortunate reference provoked renewed sobbing. Much embarrassed, I moved away to stare out across the loch. The mist was now distinctly beginning to lift, and I had been gazing out for no more than a few seconds when something attracted my eye which made me catch my breath as an electric thrill shot down my spine. I looked away, then stared again; then I turned.

'Holmes! Your telescope. Quickly!'

Holmes moved swiftly to where his coat lay and drew from a pocket his small telescope.

'What is it Watson? What do you see?'

'It's ... the monster!'

In my excitement I seized the telescope from Holmes's hand and trained it upon the loch. I had not been mistaken. Through the wreaths of mist which clung to the water, as though reluctant to part from it, a shadowy form with a long, dinosaur-like neck, glided smoothly along, its body causing a small white ripple like the bow-wave of a boat.

'There!' I cried.

Madame Valladon came to join us as Holmes seized the telescope and trained it. Even as he did so, my naked eye saw the mist swirl across like a passing cloud; and when that same patch had cleared again there was no sign of anything upon the water.

'I see nothing,' remarked Holmes dryly, snapping the telescope shut.

'It's gone,' said I, straining my eyes for another glimpse.

'If it was ever there.'

'Holmes, I swear to you. I saw it – as clearly as I see you now.'

'My dear Watson, as you so succinctly put it, we are living in the nineteenth century, not . . .'

'You doubt my word, then?'

'Let us rather say that I doubt your vision, and know of old your love for the colourful and the bizarre.'

I snorted, turning to Madame Valladon instinctively for support; but she was staring through the window, as if unseeing, her face expressionless.

'Ah, well,' I sighed. 'You were about to tell me – at least, I hope you were about to do so – what you believe caused this unfortunate lady's husband's death.'

'Asphyxiation.'

'Precisely. By drowning.'

'Not at all.'

Holmes held up the discoloured wedding ring.

'There is only one substance which could turn a copper

ring green and bleach the colour from the feathers of canaries – chlorine gas.'

'Huh!' I exclaimed. 'When it comes to figments of the imagination ... Holmes, I'll believe your theory if you'll admit that I was telling the truth just now. I did see something out there.'

'Ridiculous.'

'Nothing of the sort. I am neither drunk nor interested in promoting the local tourist trade, but I tell you ...'

'My dear Watson, we are not here to pursue phantoms or even goblins. As I have remarked before, the world is big enough for us: no ghosts need apply. Let us return to logic and to the only remaining clue we possess.'

'Which is?'

'The reference to a castle.'

He picked up the little guidebook the manager had given him and found a map of the district.

'You call for logic, Holmes,' I persisted, 'yet you yourself are the least logical of men.'

'Really? How so?'

'Because,' I replied, triumphantly thrusting my shaft home, 'you say what I saw was a figment of my imagination – although for years you have been saying that I have no imagination whatsoever.'

Holmes rolled his eyes ceilingward, appeared about to retort, but did not do so. Instead, he returned his attention to the map, muttering almost to himself, 'The question is, *which* castle?'

Once again I had cause to be impressed by Madame Valladon's resilience as, later that morning, she mounted a hired tandem and proceeded to wobble along behind Holmes, followed by myself on a tricycle, in the direction of the castle which Holmes had selected from the large number in that district for our first inspection. The mist had lifted and the sun broke through, to wink and glitter upon the calm surface of the loch beside which we pedalled. On our other hand the grassy slopes rose steeply from the road and sheep grazed unperturbed at our passing. With our cycling clothes and the picnic basket secured to my machine we might have been any carefree trio setting forth upon a day's unalloyed sight-seeing, though we carried with us an invisible load of perplexity and gloom.

Disappointment was soon to be added to our burden. The castle, rugged and gaunt as is the style in those parts, held nothing of interest for us, nor did several others which we visited in rapid succession. I was more than glad when the time came to select a choice corner of a meadow close by a road upon which to spread our repast. The sunlight was warm and the air sweet as we lay and ate, and I fancied that, in the shade of her open parasol, our tragic young friend's cheeks showed welcome indications of returning colour.

'Well,' I mused aloud, 'we have so far investigated eight draughty castles, had our bicycles attacked by sheep and our ears assaulted by bagpipes – and, in achievement, we are exactly where we started.'

'Kindly pass the cranberry sauce, *John*,' was all Holmes's reply.

As I did so I noticed figures on the roadway and recognized once again the party of seven Trappist monks, robed and cowled, trudging silently along in single file.

'I say there!' I greeted them, more to relieve my feelings than in any hope of getting a response. 'Good afternoon.'

They paid not the slightest attention to me. Madame Valladon sat up sharply and flapped her parasol open and shut in the air.

'A bee!' she cried. 'Go away, horrid thing!'

The movement must have caught the attention of the tall

leader of the monks, who turned his head and glanced at us momentarily. I recognized the lean features of the man with whom I had tried in vain to converse during our railway journey. He returned his gaze to the roadway and the dismal file tramped on and out of sight.

'Some friends of yours, Watson?' inquired Holmes, ready, no doubt, to turn my answer to some facetious use.

'Some monks,' said I.

His eyes gleamed with opportunity, but I denied him it by going on.

'I met them on the train. I tried to talk with them, but they're not allowed to speak. Trappists, you know. They just sit and meditate and study their Bibles. Matter of fact,' I added with a laugh, 'and I don't suppose you'll believe this, either, but the one I was sitting next to was reading the Book of Jonah. Odd, eh?'

Holmes's eyes remained on the direction the monks had gone.

'Quite,' was all he replied.

We were soon awheel again and making our way along a promontory which jutted craggily out into Loch Ness. At the end of it stood the remains of the mediaeval Urquhart Castle, a conglomeration of battered walls, a tower and parts of other structures, all surrounded by tumbled stones and other evidences of long years of neglect and decay. To my surprise, however, scaffolding had been erected quite extensively about the place, and I discerned the busy figures of at least two dozen workmen, evidently engaged in restoration. Amidst the rubble of a courtyard an encampment had been set up to accommodate them, with huts, tents and lines full of washing.

Reaching the approach to the gatehouse we dismounted and wheeled our machines, to halt at a closed gate and a sign reading KEEP OUT. A middle-aged man in a kilt, wearing a guide's peaked cap on his head, came hurrying towards us from the direction of the tower.

'Sorry, gentlemen. The castle is closed to the public while the work's going on.'

Holmes gazed about him.

'What is being done?'

'It's being restored by the Society for the Preservation of Scottish Monuments.'

'Too bad,' murmured Holmes. 'I particularly wanted my wife to see Urquhart Castle. The tower, I understand, is one of the most interesting examples of its kind. About 1400, if I'm not mistaken?'

'That's right,' nodded the man.

'Yes. Let me see, it was built under James the Second – or was it James the Third?'

'The Third,' answered the custodian, with a hint of impatience. 'Now, if ye can come back next year it'll all be done and I'll be glad to show ye round. Meanwhile, though . . .'

'I quite understand,' Holmes answered pleasantly. 'Come along, my dear.'

He and Madame Valladon turned their machines and wheeled them back along the way we had come, leaving me to give the man a nod and follow them. I looked back once, to see him still standing there, watching us, but when I next looked he had disappeared.

'Pleasant enough fellow,' I said, for want of anything better to remark.

'Pleasant enough,' Holmes agreed. 'But ignorant.'

'In what respect?'

He tapped the guidebook, protruding from the pocket of his Norfolk jacket.

'The tower is actually 1500 and James the Fourth.'

'Really?' said Madame Valladon, who, understandably

enough, had spoken little all day. 'But if he is an official guide, surely he should...'

'*If* he's an official guide,' Holmes answered, then suddenly stopped dead and held up his hand for us to follow suit. 'Listen!'

We were in the centre of an elevated causeway which spanned, like a bridge, the road along which we had ridden to reach this place. I obeyed Holmes's order, but could hear nothing except the loud cheeping of birds.

'Do you hear anything, Watson?'

'No. The confounded birds are making too much din.'

Holmes smiled and pointed downward.

'They're not just birds. They are old friends of ours.'

We looked down. Passing along the road, and now directly beneath us, was a canvas-topped waggon, drawn by two plodding horses. Two men, one a good deal older than the other, occupied the driving seat. I recognized them at once as the carters who had collected the cage of canaries from the old woman in that empty shop in London; and in that same instant I realized that the insistent cheeping of birds was not coming from the air about us, but from within the waggon itself, which moved on towards the castle entrance.

As we watched, the older carter pulled back on the reins and the horses stopped. The two men jumped down and went to the back of the waggon, as two men in working clothes hurried down from the castle towards them. The younger carter climbed into the back of the vehicle, drawing aside the heavy canvas covering. He handed out first a small cage of canaries, doubtless the very one we had seen them collect. His companion took it and stood waiting with the workmen as the young man struggled with something heavier in the back of the waggon. At last he was able to heave it over the tailboard into the workmen's hands. It was an open-sided wooden crate in which rested half a dozen large glass bottles, protected by wicker nests. On one of the slats of the crate I could easily read the words SULPHURIC ACID – CORROSIVE.

'Sul...? What is it?' asked Madame Valladon.

'Sulphuric acid,' said I.

'But what does it mean? The more we find out, the less sense it makes.'

'Not at all,' Holmes replied. 'To anyone who has studied chemistry it makes a great deal of sense. Sulphuric acid, when exposed to sea water, produces chlorine gas.'

I glanced at her, fearful lest his mention of the gas to which he had as good as attributed her husband's death would distress our friend into a collapse; but, brave little thing that she was, her face betrayed no hint of emotion. She was watching the workmen carrying the crate of bottles between them through the castle entrance, followed by the older carter with the canary cage. The younger man remained to secure the back of the waggon and ensure that the horses' harness was in order.

'That tower may be more interesting than I thought – and not merely architecturally,' mused Holmes aloud.

'Yes,' I agreed, 'but I think that for the, er, moment...'

I nodded towards the ruined gatehouse, from which had appeared the kilted guide, straining against the tug upon their stout leads of three enormous mastiff dogs. To my relief, Holmes took my point immediately and we resumed wheeling our bicycles along the causeway, away from the castle and its strange doings. At length we were back on the roadway and preparing to mount.

'Where, now, Holmes?'

He gave the hoped-for answer.

'Back to our hotel, for some well-earned rest and refreshment.'

'And then?'

'I suggest we wait until the evening mists roll in before we sally forth again.'

'What, ride about on these things at night? We'll get lost, for a certainty.'

'My dear Watson, I fancy your old wound has had enough cycling for one day. No, I was going to propose that we exchange these machines for a rowing-boat.'

He turned to Madame Valladon.

'Mrs. Ashdown, how would you care to go for a little boat excursion on the lake this evening?'

She sketched a charming little curtsey.

'With a fomer member of the Oxford crew, Mr. Ashdown, I should be honoured.'

So it was, early that evening, that we found ourselves out on those placid waters. As the sun had sunk rapidly towards the hills whose jagged outline formed our western horizon, the mist had begun to swirl about us and to settle on the lake's surface like steam on a simmering pot. Yet, where such a pot would have been hot to boiling point, there had clung upon us a strange chill. As usual, Holmes had refused my requests for some outline of his plans, and beyond advising me to slip my old Service revolver into my pocket before we left the hotel had given no hint of what nature of doings he anticipated; so that the chill I felt, despite the exertion of rowing, was attributable to more than the cold evening air. Whether he had confided in Madame Valladon in the privacy of their room, or whether she sensed that something dramatic and dangerous might be about to occur, I do not know; but she shivered noticeably as the sun at last disappeared and did not refuse when Holmes offered her his Norfolk jacket to place about her shoulders like a cape.

I had hoped that an oarsman of Holmes's vaunted experience would have preferred to display his skill single-handed, and I had been quite looking forward to lounging alongside a delightful companion, perhaps helping a little with the tiller as commanded, while he rowed. But in taking his position well to one side of the rower's seat, and grasping only one oar, he had made it plain that I was expected to share the labour. And hard labour it had proved to be, and no more comforting to my wound than bicycling, for, far from taking us for a pleasant little row within sight of our hotel, Holmes had promptly set a course which, after long and tiring pulling, had brought us into sight of the promontory on which we had recently stood. Keeping well away from the shore, we had rowed slowly round the point, so as to observe Urquhart Castle from every quarter. There was no sign of life about the grim pile, which loomed even more sinister in the rapidly-fading light and the rising, drifting mist.

'Holmes,' I felt impelled to complain at last, 'we've seen the castle from the front, the back, the side ... from land and from water ... What on earth now? I hope you're not proposing to spend the night out here. We shall catch our death of cold. Hah! You, too. Wouldn't it be ironic if Sherlock Holmes's last case were a case of pneumonia!'

I had intended this admittedly feeble little joke more for the benefit of the spirits of our passenger than for any other reason, yet its effect upon her was astonishing. Her eyes widened, her mouth fell open, and I saw her slender throat convulsed by a great gulp. Then I saw that she was looking not at me, but past me; and as her arm came slowly up, and a trembling finger pointed over my shoulder, I realized that she was speechless with wonder and horror.

Holmes recognized it in that same instant, and our heads turned together towards the direction she indicated. For a second the mist-swirl was all that met our eyes. Then the vaporous clouds parted – and I knew at last that my vision of a monster was no figment of the imagination.

It was several hundred yards from us, moving slowly in the same direction as we and on a parallel course. Its motion was steady, rather than undulant, its long back gleaming darkly above the water and its great, reptilian neck sticking up erectly like the prow of a Viking long-ship. I could make out little, giraffe-like horns on its crown, and round, goggling eyes. Little puffs of vapour came rhythmically from its nostrils, and it seemed to me, from that distance, that they were more of the consistency of smoke than of breath. It was an incredible sight, at once wonderful and loathsome, and I began to scramble to my feet to seek a better view. The boat rocked at my movement and I heard Madame Valladon give a little shriek, as Holmes plucked at my arm.

'Quickly, Watson. After it!'

I was jerked back into my seat by the violence with which he plunged his oar, and had to grab for mine to save it from being unshipped. Holmes's strokes had turned the head of our boat, and by the time I had regained my posture and fallen into rhythm with him we were moving on a course which would, in theory, eventually converge us upon the monster's own path, assuming that it did not outstrip us or change its direction. A quick glance over my shoulder told me that it was doing neither, and that we were, indeed, set fair to intercept it.

'Holmes,' I managed to pant, 'oughtn't we ... oughtn't we to be going *away* from it?'

'Keep rowing!' he snapped, pulling harder, thereby forcing me to do the same.

We laboured for some minutes more, before our passenger, who had been staring transfixed at the scene behind our backs, suddenly pointed again and cried, 'Look!'

Holmes and I turned together. We were just in time to see the last of the creature's humped back as it disappeared beneath the water. For some seconds only the long neck remained visible, and then it, too, sank gradually from sight, leaving no trace of its ever having been there.

'Now, Holmes,' I gasped, 'do you believe me? It's gone, just as it went this morning, but don't try to tell me now that it was never there.'

'Please be quiet,' was his ungracious answer. 'Listen.'

We sat and listened, all three of us, but heard nothing save the little slapping of the wavelets upon our boat's sides, and the indefinable stir of the great loch's waters about us. The darkness had advanced further, aided by the mist, which was beginning to assume the consistency of opaque white clouds. I was about to point out to Holmes that we should soon find ourselves benighted, and ought to make for home, when he turned to me.

'Have you your stethoscope with you, Watson?'

'Of course. I'm never without it.'

'Please give me it.'

I took off my hat and uncoiled the instrument from within the crown. Holmes almost snatched it from me, thrust the earpieces into his ears and leaned over the side of the boat, to plunge the mouth beneath the surface of the water, at the same time holding up a cautionary hand to us to keep silent. I saw Madame Valladon's anxious glance in my direction, and nodded reassuringly, giving her a little smile, which, however, she did not seem able to return.

'I can hear something,' said Holmes. 'It's coming closer.'

I saw the young woman's knuckles whiten as her hands clenched tight upon the gunwhales, and felt my own muscles tense. Gently, I unshipped my oar from its rowlock, and took a firm grip upon it with both hands, ready for anything that might eventuate.

'Nearer!' cried Holmes suddenly.

I remembered my revolver, and was just about to put the oar and drag it out when, with an almighty upheaval of the water, and a great splashing roar, the monster's head reared up into the air, not twenty yards from us. I heard Madame Valladon scream, and had a nightmare vision of the monster's repulsive neck, pouring water, and of the staring eyes and smoke-puffing nostrils – and then I found myself tipped upon my back and rolled violently into the cold water as the turbulence caught our frail craft and overturned it. I heard Madame Valladon scream again, chokingly this time, and Holmes cry out something, and then I was beneath the surface of the water and tumbling helplessly down, down into the black chill of its depths.

CHAPTER TEN

THE RED RUNNER

I HAVE recorded elsewhere the circumstances of that epic struggle between Sherlock Holmes and Professor James Moriarty upon the brink of the Richenbach Falls, above Meiringen in Switzerland, whose inescapable outcome, it seemed to me and to a sorrowing world, was that neither of the combatants could have survived. As a rejoicing world was subsequently to learn, one of them did, miraculously, escape death; and that one was not Professor Moriarty. Holmes lived, to be able to tell me how he had managed to avoid falling into that dread chasm at all; but had he done so, had he plunged, like his rival, into that fearful cauldron of swirling water and seething foam from which there could have been no escape, he must have felt much as I did as I was sucked inexorably towards the bottom of Loch Ness on that night.

They say that a drowning man's past life flashes across his mind in his last moments, but I cannot agree. All that occupied the turmoil that was my mind was the desperate wish to save myself: I was too busy with practicalities to contemplate the spiritual or the metaphysical. I struck out with my arms, lashed with my legs, fought with the power of my shoulders against the pressure that was drawing me down; and, for some reason of which I am not quite sure, I cried: 'Help!'

'Over here, Watson,' replied the voice of Sherlock Holmes.

That the corporeal spirit of Holmes, rather than any Heavenly emissary, should attend my passing seemed, in that instant of recognition, to be both comforting and fitting. For years we had shared danger, excitement, pleasure and accommodation, and, for all our differences of personality and opinion, could scarcely have been closer to one another, even had we been kin. I had time to hope that, as he, too, went down for the last time, he would be conscious of my presence and would acknowledge it as kindly as I did his.

'Watson, do hold on to her, man!' came Holmes's voice again, somewhat petulantly, I thought, in the circumstances.

It was then that I discovered that perhaps the principal reason for the blackness which was all about me was that my eyes were tightly shut. I opened them. Immediately before me bobbed the angelic, yet decidedly mortal, face of Madame Gabrielle Valladon. I paddled across to her and she placed her hands on my shoulders.

'Are you all right?' I asked, surprised to hear my voice.

'Yes, thank you. But I lost my parasol.'

Behind her I could see the hump of our upturned boat, to the far side of which clung Holmes. Treading water, I guided our companion to the hull and we held on.

'Holmes ...' I began, emotion-charged words forming themselves in my mind. 'I thought I ... we ... were ...'

'From the way you were threshing about, Watson, anyone might have thought you were drowning,' he replied. 'Look at that.'

He pointed beyond us, and we turned to look. Although darkness was coming quickly now, the mist had cleared again temporarily and Castle Urquhart on its promontory was visible in all its detail, even to the slender rods of the scaffolding which enshrouded the tower. To my astonishment, as I blinked and looked again, that framework of scaffolding was rising slowly into the air. All three of us watched it in silence, as it rose higher and still higher, above the top of the tower. There it paused for some moments, and then, equally slowly, began to descend, until it was once more back in its original place, and, as if arranged, the mist had swirled in finally, obscuring the castle and the land on which it stood from our view.

'What on earth...?'

'My guess,' said Holmes, 'is that the monster, after a hard day's work, has returned home for his supper – an example which I suggest we might emulate.'

Without much difficulty he and I righted our boat and I clambered in first, to help them both aboard. We were bedraggled, but thankful, and cheerful to be in no worse state, and the row back to our hotel seemed to take far less time than the outward journey had done. I prescribed a brisk towelling, a change of clothing and brandy and soda for all, and within an hour of our mishap we were gathered, fully restored, in 'Mr. and Mrs. Ashdown's' room.

Madame Valladon lay on her bed, clad in a warm dressing-gown and clearly sleepy from the effects of the warmth and the brandy after her chill exertions. Holmes and I had both changed into fresh suits. I was thankful to sit beside the fire, while he paced, pausing frequently to peer out at what little could still be discerned of the mist-shrouded loch. For all his laconic manner, he evidently shared my relief at our narrow escape, for he whistled softly as he paced. I was surprised to recognize the tune as the main theme from *Swan Lake*.

'Holmes,' said I, 'no one knows better than I how loath you are to communicate your full plans to any other person until the instant of their fulfilment, but I believe Madame Valladon will agree with me when I say that this is one occasion when we are entitled to insist.'

To my surprise, he stopped, turned, smiled, and said, 'I quite agree, my dear Watson.'

It would have been characteristic of him if he had then ushered me from the room and not addressed me again until he had occasion to demand the coffee pot over our next day's breakfast table; but for once he seemed in communicative mood.

'It is nothing new, actually,' he began. 'As a rule, when I have gained some slight indication of the course of events I am able to guide myself by the thousands of other similar cases which occur to my memory.'

'Holmes,' I interrupted, furrowing my brow, 'of all the cases on which I've accompanied you, I don't recall thousands which have involved the Loch Ness Monster and a castle whose scaffolding goes up and down like the Army and Navy Stores lift. Come to think of it, I don't remember a single one.'

'Perhaps not. Yet we *have* come across this situation before.'

'We have? Where?'

'At the ballet. There was a lake and a castle. There was a swan that turns out to be not really a swan – or, in this case, a monster that isn't really a monster.'

'Ah!' I conceded.

He nodded acknowledgment.

'Tell me, Watson, what is it that feeds on canaries and sulphuric acid, and has machinery for a heart?'

'Is this a conundrum, Holmes?'

'Not at all. It is a perfectly serious inquiry.'

I enmeshed the gears of my brain, but it was the reclining figure upon the bed who answered him.

'An engine?'

He clapped his hands a little, in mock applause.

'The stethoscope is a very sensitive instrument, and water is an excellent conductor of sound. There is no doubt at all that we are dealing with a mechanical monster.'

'Great heavens, Holmes!'

'Not only is it equipped with an artificial heart – it also has artificial lungs. Judging from the bubbles on the surface of the lake – what, you didn't notice them? – it uses some form of air pump.'

Madame Valladon was sitting upright now.

'You think my husband was involved in all this – because he was an engineer?'

'I am sure of it.'

'But why,' I intervened, 'would anybody build a mechanical monster? Surely, not to attract tourists.'

'I doubt it.'

'To frighten people?'

'Not very likely.'

'Then ...'

But Madame Valladon had a more pressing question.

'Why did they try to keep me from finding my husband? And why was he buried anonymously?'

'I believe I have a pretty good notion of what they were – or are – up to,' Holmes replied.

'They?'

'The Society for the Preservation of Scottish Monuments. Come in!'

There had come a knock at the door. The hotel manager entered, carrying a magnum of champagne.

'Ah, Mr. Ashdown. Here is your bottle of champagne.'

'I ordered no champagne.'

'No, indeed. You are to deliver it.'

He handed the bottle to Holmes.

'Am I, indeed?'

'Those are my instructions, sir.'

'And to whom am I to deliver it?'

'That I can't say, sir. But the carriage is waiting for you downstairs.'

The manager withdrew with a bow. Having perused the label on the bottle and evidently learnt nothing from it, Holmes rose and put on his cape and took up his deerstalker.

'Watson, you had better stay here with Gab ... with Madame Valladon.'

'Certainly not, Holmes,' I said. 'Madame Valladon will be safer here behind a locked door than you will be, God knows where, with a bottle of champagne.'

He glanced inquiringly at our friend, who was again lying back on the bed.

'I should like to accompany you, Mr. Holmes,' she murmured drowsily, 'but I am already so tired. I do not think ...'

'Quite so,' he responded. 'But to make doubly sure of your security I am going to lock this door from the outside.'

'That will not be necessary.'

'I trust not. If it is, then I shall never forgive myself for not having done it. Rest well, my dear, and let us hope that all this sorry business will have been cleared up by the time we return.'

Taking my coat and hat, having paused only to stuff fresh, dry cartridges into my revolver, I nodded paternally to her and left the room. Holmes locked the door and put the key in his pocket and together we went downstairs. There seemed to be few people about in the hotel, but I noticed the manager watch us leave and my thoughts lingered anxiously for a moment on the defenceless creature we were leaving behind, and on the tragedy and danger which she had already had to experience in this strange and disturbing business. Holmes saw my hesitation and shook his head firmly, beckoning me to follow, and, trusting in his instinct, which I had so seldom known to fail, I followed him out of the door, to where a gig stood at the foot of the steps.

The driver of the gig, I was astonished to see, was the kilted man whom we had last seen as the purported custodian to Urquhart Castle. He made no move to get down and open the door for us. Holmes marched forward and looked up at the man.

'Where are we going?'

The driver merely eased himself in his seat and took up the reins.

'Ye'd best be getting in. It's late already.'

Holmes shrugged and climbed up. He flourished the bottle.

'Some sort of party, no doubt?'

The man smiled in a way I did not altogether care for.

'Ye'll not be disappointed in the guest list.'

'Who is our host?' I asked.

He flicked the reins.

'Jonah,' he said; and at a smart trot we left the hotel grounds and were out upon the road leading to Urquhart Castle.

As we drove I was conscious of the mist-hung expanse of the loch stretched on our one hand, and of the hills looming on the other. I shrank against the chill air into my heavy coat, and more than once fingered my revolver, praying that it might still work after its earlier soaking. Holmes brooded impassively, our driver remained grim and uncommunicative and none of us spoke any word.

The castle, as we neared it, wore a new and if anything

more eerie appearance. The flickering flames of torches showed yellow against the ancient masonry and shadows darted to and fro as people moved beneath the ruins. The gate which had barred us from entrance earlier had been opened and we were evidently well expected, for we bowled through without challenge, passed under the arch of the gatehouse and gained the inner courtyard, where we pulled up sharply with a final clatter of hooves and rasp of wheels. The driver jumped down and we followed suit.

'This way,' he ordered.

I glanced at Holmes and noted that he was holding the big bottle in a way which would have made it instantly useful as a club, if needed. Keeping my hand on the revolver in my pocket, I strode after him, darting glances from side to side, instinctively watching the black, wavering shadows for any movement which might spell a threat.

At the top of some steps we found our feet upon softer ground, and, looking down, I was surprised to find that it was red carpeting, a large roll of which two workmen were unwinding ahead of us in the direction of the tower. The red runner! Could this be our final clue, and could it be about to lead us to something, or someone, who would solve our mystery for us, perhaps by an act of violence that would by its nature make plain his interest in our investigation and, albeit perhaps too late for us to act upon it, explain the singular events of the past few days?

Raising my eyes to where the workmen had finished unrolling the carpet, I saw a tall figure outlined against a tent, to whose entrance the carpet ran. The light behind him made him seem enormous, far more than normal human size, and its flickering made his silhouette loom and lean and sway, although as we drew closer I could see that he was standing rock still, his hands clasped rigidly behind his frock-coated back. He watched us halt before him, seemed, almost without moving his eyes, to examine us from head to foot, and then, at last, spoke.

'Welcome to the castle, gentlemen.'

'Good evening, Mycroft,' Holmes replied.

CHAPTER ELEVEN

V.R.

I REMEMBER Sherlock Holmes once remarking to me something to the effect that to meet his brother Mycroft anywhere outside the territory bounded by his Pall Mall lodgings, the Diogenes Club, and Whitehall, would be akin to encountering a tramcar coming down a country lane. I can only say that had I been faced, there on that red carpet beneath the lowering, torchlit shape of an ancient castle on the shore of Loch Ness, with a No. 7 omnibus, the billiard-marker from my club and the manager of Fortnum and Mason, all together, I should scarcely have felt more surprise than I did to recognize the elegant figure who screwed his monocle more securely into place and traversed us both with a broad smile. As ever, my companion appeared to be quite nonplussed. He pointed casually to the carpet.

'Really, Mycroft, you shouldn't have gone to all this trouble just for me.'

'It is not for you, Sherlock; and I hope your shoes are clean.'

Holmes gave a little bow.

'I should certainly not wish to despoil the *red runner*.'

His brother beamed even more broadly and outstretched a hand towards the bottle of champagne in Holmes's grasp.

'I'll take that.'

I felt my muscles tense again as I watched for Holmes's next move; but he merely passed across the bottle, remarking, 'Not a very good vintage, I fear.'

'Mediocre,' Mycroft agreed. 'However, it's not for drinking.'

He turned to the kilted man, who lurked at his elbow.

'Tie it up, MacGregor.'

For a split second I believed he had said, 'Tie them up,' and my revolver was half out of my pocket before I realized he was referring in some obscure way to the champagne, which he had passed to the man. I fancy Mycroft saw my movement, and I fully expected him to order me to hand over the weapon. But he merely indicated the entrance to the tent before which he stood, and said, 'In here.' Taking my cue from Holmes, I followed.

My immediate impression of the tent's interior was of an engineering workshop. On every hand, on trestle tables and on the floor itself, lay pieces of machinery – flywheels, rods, shafts, cylinder casings, and so forth. But as I glanced about, in the light from the single paraffin lamp which hung from the tent pole, I observed other items, some of them familiar enough to make me stare.

There was a small bed, or cot, with its bedding secured in a roll. Beside it lay a small trunk, on which was painted the name VALLADON. On the trunk stood a photograph of a woman, in a silver frame. Nearby lay Madame Valladon's parasol, looking somewhat bedraggled after its immersion in the loch, and a stethoscope which I recognized at once as my own.

Mycroft Holmes wheeled round, his face now stern.

'Despite my most emphatic warning, Sherlock, you have persisted in meddling. It would have served you right if you had all been drowned.'

'Sorry to be so unobliging,' murmured my friend.

Mycroft glowered at him and gesticulated towards the parasol and stethoscope.

'I imagine this belongs to the pretty lady . . . and that to your "valet". We recovered them from the loch.'

'Ah, yes,' Holmes replied. 'Speaking of things in the loch. . . .'

Mycroft Holmes stepped a pace closer to him, to peer intently into his face.

'How much do you know – or think you know?'

'Of the two, let me rather tell you what I think I know. I think you are testing some sort of underwater vessel, disguised as a monster to mislead the gullible. I think it is an experimental model, operated by a crew of midgets.'

'A midget submarine!' I could not help exclaiming. The brothers Holmes turned as one to give me a look which made me wish I had kept silent.

'I think,' Holmes resumed at length, 'that it is powered by sulphuric acid batteries, and carries canaries aboard to detect escaping gas. In short, it is altogether a unique contraption.'

'Not quite unique,' his brother disagreed. 'At this moment four countries are trying to develop what we term' (with a cold glance at me) 'a submersible. So far, none of them has been able to solve the critical problem – how to keep it submerged long enough for it to be effective.'

'What does the Good Book say? "And Jonah lived in the belly of that fish for three days and three nights." '

'Very good, Sherlock. Yes, that was our goal; and, thanks to Valladon's air pump, we have been able to draw ahead of our competitors. It is a highly complex system of filtration, which necessitated a series of trials . . .'

'And at least one error.'

Mycroft nodded seriously.

'During a test in the Moray Firth, pressure caused a leak in the hull. Sea water got in and mixed with the acid in the batteries, to produce chlorine gas. Before they could surface,

Valladon and two of the crew were dead.'

'So you had them buried in unmarked graves, to preserve your secret.'

Mycroft nodded again. Holmes turned to me.

'You see, Watson, what lengths the Diogenes Club will go to?'

'The Diog...!'

If I was surprised at this, I was to be amazed by what followed.

'It was essential to keep the information from your client,' insisted Mycroft Holmes. His brother raised an eyebrow.

'You went to all those lengths to prevent Madame Valladon from finding her husband?'

'Your client isn't Madame Valladon. I would not accuse you of having realized it, Sherlock, but you have been working for the Imperial German Government. It is they who were seeking this Belgian engineer – or rather, his invention. They knew he was employed by us, but they were unable to discover where, so they enlisted you, the best brain in England – modesty forbade me to say the *second* best brain – to help them. You, my dear brother, have been working for the Wilhelmstrasse.'

Even Sherlock Holmes appeared nonplussed for a moment at this.

'But Madame Valladon...?' I asked.

'She is dead. The Germans disposed of her three weeks ago, in Brussels.'

He picked up the silver framed photograph.

'This is, or was, Gabrielle Valladon.'

There was no resemblance between the woman whose portrait I saw and the one whom we had left behind at our hotel. Mycroft Holmes continued.

'The woman who was brought to you in the middle of the

night, apparently fished out of the Thames and suffering from loss of – memory, is, in fact, one Ilse von Hoffmannsthal, one of Germany's most accomplished agents.'

I felt a sudden pang of compassion for my friend. He had picked up the parasol and was twirling it between his hands, opening and shutting it nervously, as if humiliated by this disclosure of how he had been duped. His brother continued remorselessly.

'They planted her upon you quite neatly, so that you would lead them to their objective, the air pump. It was, if you will forgive my saying so, very much like using a pig to find truffles.'

I could have stepped forward to demand that he retract this slurring comparison, and half expected to see the battle signals fly in my friend's own face. But he merely shrugged and tossed the parasol down. Mycroft Holmes took out his watch.

'More visitors?' I demanded curtly.

He snapped his watch shut and returned it to his fob.

'*A* visitor, at any rate,' he smiled, 'whose initials, I fancy, will be instantly recognizable to you. My deplorable brother here inscribed them in bullet holes in your sitting-room wall, I'm told.'

The initials V.R. were, indeed, inscribed (though, I am happy to add, not in bullet holes) upon the doors of the splendid coach which, a little later, we watched approaching the castle. As it came nearer, we observed that a crown surmounted the initials, and another adorned the top of the coach. A handsomely-liveried coachman and footman rode behind the four superb white horses, and two dignified outriders trotted beside. The carriage lamps were lit and the curtains drawn.

Holmes, his brother and I waited with half a dozen well-dressed men of intellectual aspect whom Mycroft had introduced to us as scientists engaged in the development of the submersible craft. With bated breath, I watched the magnificent vehicle draw up at the foot of the red-carpeted steps. The footman sprang down to open the door nearest us, and handed out a tiny figure.

Her Majesty Queen Victoria, Defender of the Faith, Empress of India, was less than five feet tall, and so stout in proportion that she appeared almost spherical. Yet an incomparable dignity and a grace of movement strange in one of such build utterly transcended these physical disadvantages and the fact that her small face was also overplump and set in lines of habitual sorrow and disappointment. She was clad all in black, as she had been since the death so many years before of her adored husband, the Prince Consort. A bonnet reminiscent of a widow's coif covered her severely-parted grey hair and was secured at the back and under her chin by a large bow of black silk, in whose tying there was no hint of feminine coquetry. A richly-trimmed black dolman covered her shoulders. Simple pearl earrings were her only jewellery.

I was too young to remember those days of which my father had told me, when, at her Coronation and marriage, she had appeared a fairy princess of spun-sugar and rose petals; and the later time when she had charmed visitors to the Great Exhibition of 1851 as a blooming, happy wife and mother. Only the pale clear complexion and the proud little Roman nose remained of that young Queen in this woman whose sixty-nine years might, by her appearance, have been seventy-nine. Yet, in her presence, there was a calm majesty which brought into Holmes's eyes a look such as I had never seen there before; and into my own, I confess, a tear.

Mycroft left us and descended the red-carpeted steps, to bow low before her.

'Your Majesty,' we heard him murmur.

She extended a small, gloved hand, which he touched.

'I trust you had a pleasant journey, Ma'am.'

'It was long and it was tedious,' answered the Queen. I had not heard her voice before and had always fancied that, with her Germanic ancestry, it would be accented in the way that her son's, the Prince of Wales's, was said to be. It was not, however, though there was a precision to the enunciation which somehow betrayed that the speaker's background was not native English. There was also no doubting the crisp authority and strong will of this little old lady.

'We trust this visit is going to prove worth our while, Mr. Holmes.'

Mycroft bowed again.

'I can assure you, Ma'am, it will be.'

A lady-in-waiting and a uniformed equerry had by now alighted from the coach. The party formed itself into a little procession and came up the steps towards us, led by the Queen and Mycroft, who towered above her.

'Now, Mr. Holmes,' said the Queen, 'what is this curious ship we have been invited to christen?'

'We call it a submersible, Ma'am. It travels under water.'

'Under water? What a fantastic idea.'

They had reached the steps and Mycroft was directing her attention to the men who stood beside us.

'Ma'am, may I present some of the engineers and scientists who have been responsible for this achievement? Mr. J. W. Ferguson, naval architect...'

The men bowed in turn.

'Professor Simpson, our leading expert on hydraulics...

Mr. W. W. Prescott, co-inventor of the revolving periscope...'

'We do not claim to understand your achievements in the way our dear departed husband would have done,' the Queen told them, 'but England is proud of you, gentlemen. To think that man is at last to be enabled to observe the fishes in their native habitat, and to extend his knowledge of underwater plants and coral reefs...'

I noticed Mycroft looking somewhat uncomfortable at this, and heard him clear his throat, as if it would serve as a tactful interruption; but the Queen had passed on and had come to where Holmes and I stood.

'And what was your contribution to this enterprise, young man?' she asked Holmes as he bowed.

'I am afraid, Ma'am, a rather negligible one,' he answered, and I wondered what I should answer if asked the same question. The Queen turned to Mycroft with a look of inquiry in her face.

'This is my brother, Sherlock, Your Majesty.'

Her expression was instantly transformed.

'Ah, yes! Mr. Sherlock Holmes.'

Holmes bowed again.

'We have been following your exploits with great interest. Are you engaged upon one of your fascinating investigations at the moment?'

'In a manner of speaking, Ma'am.'

'When may we expect to read Dr. Watson's account of it?'

'I hope never, Ma'am,' Holmes answered. 'It has not been one of my more successful endeavours.'

She glanced at him searchingly, and I saw Mycroft about to guide her to me, and was preparing to make my bow, when a bagpipes began to caterwaul nearby and the Queen turned away from us.

'Ah, I take it the ceremonies are about to begin,' she said to Mycroft. 'Now, where is this underwater ship of yours?'

Mycroft pointed to the tower.

'In the dungeons, Ma'am.'

'The dungeons!' I was surprised by the sudden gaiety of her silvery laugh, in such contrast to the severity of her customary expression. Briskly for her years and all-enveloping dress, she moved away along the red carpet, Mycroft hastening to fall in beside her and the rest of us to tag along behind her attendants. At the entrance to the tower the kilted custodian was waiting. He bowed deeply and stepped aside as our procession passed.

A spiral iron staircase, upon which our feet rang eerily in that cavernous acoustic, led us down into a vast, rough-hewn chamber; dungeon enough, I thought, for half a battalion. The floor had been concreted, to slope gradually into a ramp, whose lower reaches, I noticed, were awash with water and gave access to the loch. Despite the gloom, I could just make out the camouflage of vegetation-hung scaffolding at the outer entrance.

On the upper part of the ramp rested a vessel of a type completely strange to me. It was something of a cross between a cigar and a marrow in shape, its body constructed of strong metal plates bound together by row upon row of thousands of rivets, whose pattern gave an effect of ribbing, or the buttoning of a leather-upholstered chair. There were no portholes, and access seemed to be gained by a hatch in the top, whose metal cover stood open on strong hinges. Part of the hull at either side was shaped as a tube, from which protruded, pointing the same way as the strange vessel's bows, an ugly-looking device resembling for all the world an elongated artillery shell, though what these could have to do with the observation of fish or the study of coral reefs I could not imagine.

A metal plate, similar to those on the sides of railway locomotives, was fastened to the vessel's side, bearing the name H.M.S. *Jonah*. Dangling by a rope at the prow was our bottle of champagne.

The most remarkable feature of the strange scene, however, was the activity which was in progress on the top – or, I supposed, the deck – of the submersible. Clad in woollen jerseys and naval caps, four diminutive figures were hauling upon a chain. They were clearly the four surviving midgets, whom we had observed mourning at the graveside of their brothers; and at the other end of the chain, being gradually lifted roofwards, was the long neck and head of the 'monster', which, I could easily see, had until a few minutes before been attached to the vessel's prow.

As we neared the foot of the staircase a voice barked an order and there came the clash of boots in naval precision as a party of sailors sprang to attention behind their officer and stood rigidly, staring almost unseeing at their Queen as she passed by.

Mycroft gesticulated towards the craft.

'There she is, Ma'am. Her Majesty's Ship *Jonah*.'

The Queen's attention was focused upon the monster's head.

'And what, may we ask, is the purpose of that hideous gargoyle at a Royal Naval occasion?'

'Merely a decoy, Ma'am,' replied Mycroft, smiling suavely.

'Oh, I see. To frighten away the sharks?'

Mycroft beamed.

'Something of the sort, Ma'am.'

He made some sort of signal to the midgets, who had finished hauling the monstrous appendage clear.

'The crew will now demonstrate the working of the submersible, Ma'am,' said he.

The midgets were scrambling into the hatchway atop the vessel. The Queen turned to Mycroft.

'Aren't they rather small for sailors?'

'They are, Ma'am. But, because of the limited space available in the craft, the Navy made an exception.'

'They should make it a rule,' declared the Queen. 'It is quite fatiguing to pin on all those medals while standing on our toes.'

I wondered whether it was in order to laugh openly at this Royal Joke, but observing the equerry and lady-in-waiting to be merely smiling and shaking silently I contented myself with doing the same. It was now plain from Mycroft's gestures that the Queen was being invited to enter the vessel herself, and after a moment's hesitation she did so. Mycroft signified that we might follow, and as we did I felt the vibration of the engines being started.

It was no easy matter for us all to squeeze into the confinement of that metal tube, and, having achieved it, no pleasant experience being there. All was noise and ordered confusion. Machinery throbbed, clattered and hissed, as metal rods rose and fell into bottles of sulphuric acid, shafts turned, wheels raced, and great bellows inflated and deflated. The midgets scurried everywhere, oiling, examining, adjusting, turning handwheels, pulling switches and operating, for the Queen's benefit, what I took to be a sort of periscope. Above our heads I noticed a small cage full of chirping canaries, and had no doubt that I had seen it and them not many hours before.

Above the noise I could hear Mycroft explaining to the Queen.

'These are the batteries. The engines are powerful enough to enable the vessel to travel underwater at a speed of two knots... The ballast tanks, which allow it to submerge and rise again... The air pump which filters and recirculates the air... The periscope for scanning the surface of the water...'

'Yes, yes,' said the Queen, who appeared to be searching the metal floor for something, and I hoped for one moment that I might have the memorable privilege of finding and restoring a Royal Glove.

'Ma'am?' inquired Mycroft, seeing her attention distracted.

'Where is the glass bottom?'

'The...?'

'The glass bottom – through which to see the fish.'

'That, er, is not quite the, er, idea, Ma'am,' Mycroft replied.

'I beg your pardon, Mr. Holmes?'

'Observing fish, Ma'am. That is not, er, quite the purpose.'

'Then, pray, what *is* the purpose?'

'H.M.S. *Jonah*, Ma'am, is being commissioned as a warship.'

The Queen's already prominent eyes bulged even more.

'A warship!'

She waved a hand violently.

'Stop that noise. Stop it!'

A hasty signal from Mycroft was relayed by the naval officer to the crew, who ran about even more frenziedly, and in a moment the vibrations shuddered away to nothing.

'You had better explain, Mr. Holmes,' said Queen Victoria, and her voice rang alarmingly in the now-quiet metal chamber. Mycroft's manner, however, was deferential but undaunted.

'The Admiralty regards this craft as the ultimate weapon in naval warfare, Ma'am. It can seek out and destroy enemy ships while remaining completely invisible.

'You mean it can fire at other vessels while under water?'

'Precisely, Ma'am. Your Majesty may have noticed the shell-like projectiles protruding from the tubes outside? Those are the torpedoes, fired by means of these levers here. They have been proved accurate up to as far as one hundred and twenty feet.'

'But, if I understand you correctly, Mr. Holmes, these torpedoes would be fired while the vessel is submerged, and therefore without warning.'

'That is correct, Ma'am.'

'And without the vessel showing its colours?'

'Indeed, Ma'am.'

Even Mycroft's composure was obviously shaken by the vehemence of the Queen's next utterance.

'Mr. Holmes, we are not amused.'

'Not...? I... I beg your...'

'It is unsportsmanlike, it is un-English, and it is in very poor taste. We will have none of it.'

'But, Ma'am...'

'Sometimes, and this is one of them, we despair of the state of the world. What will these ... these scientists think of next?'

There was a general shuffling of feet around me, and a glance showed me the scientists' discomfort. I squared my shoulders and did my best not to look as though I was one of them.

Mycroft urged, 'Ma'am, the state of the world is precisely the point at issue. At this very moment the German Count von Zeppelin is experimenting with a dirigible...'

'And what, pray, is a dirigible?'

'A rigid balloon, Ma'am, which could fly over London and drop a bomb on Buckingham Palace, if it chose. It is being developed at the express order of the Kaiser.'

'Willie, my grandson, do a thing like that to us? Nonsense! We refuse to believe it.'

'We have conclusive proof, Ma'am. Our agent in Friedrichshafen, a man named Ibbetson, actually saw the dirigible and made a drawing of it. Unfortunately, the poor fellow was apprehended before he could cross the border.'

'Nevertheless,' said the Queen emphatically, indicating her surroundings, 'we do not wish any part of this beastly invention. Get rid of it. What do you say? – scuttle it. The sooner the better.'

Mycroft was visibly perspiring.

'May I point out, Ma'am . . .'

'You may not, Mr. Holmes. And do not concern yourself about that dirigible dropping bombs on Buckingham Palace. We shall write a very sharp note to the Kaiser about that matter. A very sharp note indeed.'

She turned her back abruptly upon Mycroft, and addressed her equerry.

'And now we wish to return to Balmoral.'

As the Queen's party mounted the spiral staircase leading from the chamber, Mycroft, this time, was left to trail with his brother and myself in the wake of the others.

'Well, Mycroft,' said Holmes, 'it seems we've both been undone by a woman. A shame, too. All that superb engineering, and all that cunning espionage, for what? Nothing!'

Mycroft paused for a moment, and looked down at the metal craft, whose crew now stood about uncertainly, their occupation gone.

'I'm not so sure, Sherlock,' he said slowly. 'If the Germans want the thing so badly . . .'

'Well?'

'Sherlock, may I ask you to do something for me?'

'Only too delighted, Mycroft.'

'Since you are on such intimate terms with Fräulein von Hoffmannsthal . . .'

A guarded look came into Holmes's face.

'Ye-es?'

Mycroft gestured towards the rest of the party.

'We must at least see Her Majesty off the premises. Then I will explain.'

We hurried in the wake of the party into the chill of the night air, where the bagpipes' yelp and whine made an unwittingly appropriate comment upon the fiasco we had just witnessed, and watched our Sovereign Lady take her departure without so much as a backward glance.

CHAPTER TWELVE

ILSE VON HOFFMANNSTHAL

AFTER Her Majesty had gone, Mycroft drew Holmes out of earshot of myself or anyone else and for fully fifteen minutes they conversed together, wearing the most serious expressions. Finally, they appeared to reach agreement and shook hands upon it, after which they came back to where I was waiting, preoccupied now with thoughts of the night's sleep I had missed and vowing that I would wreak my revenge upon the breakfast table. We took our parting, but as Mycroft walked away towards the tower Holmes called after him to ask if I might retrieve my stethoscope from the tent.

'By all means, my dear fellow,' called his brother, evidently now in high good humour.

We stepped into the tent, and once more I coiled the instrument into my hat. Holmes picked up Madame Valladon's parasol.

'At any rate, Watson, she might as well have her parasol, wouldn't you say?'

'Holmes, if what your brother told us is true...'

'Oh, it is. If Mycroft doesn't know a thing, or hasn't deduced it from what he does know, then he doesn't utter it.'

'Well, then, what is going to happen to her? And the submersible? What of it?'

His reply was characteristically infuriating.

'My dear Watson, unless I am much mistaken those

streaks of faint light to the east there signify that dawn is in the offing. I am sure that the unexpected excitement of this royal occasion has more than compensated you for the loss of your sleep, but I can imagine the keenness with which you are anticipating your next assault upon our hotel's catering resources. I suggest we return there without further delay.'

'But Holmes ... !'

'There is also an admirable view of the loch from the windows, and my telescope is at present lying on my dressing-table. Come.'

The kilted guide drove us to our hotel in the gig in which he had fetched us. Dawn was advancing rapidly by the time we arrived, and as the gig rattled away once more in the direction of the castle Holmes paused in front of the hotel, thoughtfully staring up at the windows of his room and twirling the parasol in his hands. I need scarcely remark that I was none the wiser than I had been at the castle. Every one of my entreaties that he should outline his plans had been turned aside with a quip, an irrelevancy, or, most aggravating of all, silence.

We went up through the sleeping hotel to his room. He inserted the key in the lock, and grunted with satisfaction at finding the door still secure. The curtains were not fully closed, and enough of the faint dawn light was seeping in to reveal the girl we had known as Madame Valladon in her bed, dressed in the pink negligée with the maribou feathers. Her blonde hair was spread enchantingly about her pillow, and her expression was more that of an innocent child than of an agent of one of the most determined and ruthless espionage organizations that the world had ever known. The conflicting emotions of sympathy for her as a woman, admiration for her bravery, and contempt for her as an enemy of our country welled within me and merged into a feeling of heavy-heartedness and distaste, and a longing to return to the honest familiarity of Baker Street.

After regarding her for some moments, Holmes crossed quietly to the windows, which led on to a small balcony. He opened the window and glanced out, and I could tell from the stiffening of his shoulders that something had attracted his interest. I crossed to join him, but he soundlessly barred my way and pushed me back out of the line of sight from outside. He had not prevented me, however, from seeing what he had seen: the seven Trappist monks, led as usual by the tallest, were standing some little way off, silhouetted against the gleaming loch water. They appeared to be watching the hotel intently.

To my surprise, Holmes swung the parasol casually yet deliberately, so that its point struck against a metal lamp shade. The sound awoke her in an instant and she struggled on to one elbow, brushing hair and sleep from her eyes. She smiled when she recognized us, but something in our expressions, no doubt, caused the smile to fade.

'I am sorry if we startled you,' Holmes said in more formal tones than he was accustomed to use when addressing her. 'Since you're up though, perhaps you could tell me the German word for castle? *Schloss*, isn't it?'

I could distinctly detect a new wariness in her eyes as she answered carefully, 'I think so.'

'Thank you. And how would one say "under the castle"? *Unter das Schloss*? Or is it *die Schloss*?'

She began to get out of bed.

'I do not know. My German is not so good.'

Holmes shrugged. 'Isn't it? Oh, by the way, your Trappist friends are lined up out there, waiting to hear from you. It's a chilly morning, and we don't wish to keep them standing about any longer than is necessary – do we, Fräulein von Hoffmannsthal?'

For a long moment she stood there facing us expressionless, as no doubt her trained mind raced to determine her next move. Obviously, there was none.

'*Unter dem Schloss*,' she said flatly.

'Thank you,' said Holmes cheerfully, and held up the parasol. 'Here is your signalling device – a trifle damp after floating in the loch, I'm afraid, but let us hope effective, nevertheless.'

He offered it to her.

'Would you care to let your friends know where they can find the submersible?'

She made no move.

'No? Then I shall just have to do it myself. Let us hope my memory of the Morse code is adequate for the purpose.'

He returned to the window, and, standing well to one side, where he himself would be out of sight to the watchers, he thrust out the parasol and began to jerk it open and shut in the way that I had seen its owner do in what I had taken for mere nervous fiddling. I was under no such misapprehension now, as I watched the deliberately long and short jerks with which Holmes signalled to the men outside, and it flashed back to my mind that the occasions when I had seen Madame Valladon apparently toying with her parasol in this manner had been on the railway station at Inverness, when the Trappists had been crossing the bridge within our sight, and again during our picnic, when they had passed along the road. I looked at her, marvelling at the cool duplicity of which one so essentially feminine could be capable. She caught my glance, and gave me a slow, resigned smile; but I could not return it.

'*Unter dem Schloss*,' said Holmes, as he finished signalling and stepped back into the room. Taking care not to be spotted I peeped round the curtains and saw the party of monks moving rapidly away along the loch shore in the direction of Urquhart Castle.

'Well, Fräulein,' I heard Holmes say, 'you can consider your part of the mission accomplished. It is up to the monks now.'

I could see the surprise on her face, and must say that I shared it.

'You've ... you've sent them to the castle, Holmes? But they'll ...'

'Walk into a trap,' Ilse von Hoffmannsthal corrected what I had been about to say. My surprise was redoubled then to hear Holmes answer 'They will encounter surprisingly little resistance. It will take only a small bottle of chloroform to overcome the guard.'

She stared without speaking for a moment

'You mean you are going to let them have the air pump?'

'Better than that. They may have the submersible itself. They will find it with its engines running, all ready to go. I assume they're all expert sailors? I imagined as much. And since my information is that there is a German battleship cruising off the coast of Scotland waiting to make a rendezvous with them at sea ...'

He broke off.

'John ... or I should say Watson, now that Mr. and Mrs. Ashdown have decided to divorce and will no longer be needing a valet's services ... Watson, my dear fellow, I suggest you get your things for our departure and join me here again in about an hour's time.'

'Dammit, Holmes!' I was impelled to cry, and even if the woman had not been a spy my emotions were such that I should still have used the word before her. 'You're not going to get away this time without telling me what your game is. As ... as an Englishman concerned for his country's security, I *demand* to know.'

He laid his hand on my shoulder.

'So you shall, my dear Watson, so you shall. As I said, if you will return in about an hour's time ...' He turned to the woman. 'I suggest you commence your packing, too, Fräulein. Mycroft will be here presently to take you into custody.'

'Who *is* this Mycroft?'

'Forgive me. You haven't met, but he knows all about you. He is my brother and also a founder member of the Diogenes Club, of which I am sure your efficient masters in Germany have told you.'

'Your Secret Service?'

'Not the whole of it, though, in relation to its size, a particularly influential part.'

I could sense the resignation in her as she lifted her suitcase and placed it on the bed.

'And you?' she addressed Holmes. 'I never had you deceived for one moment, did I? You knew right from the beginning – from the moment the cabbie brought me to your rooms.'

She turned to look at me as she crossed to the wardrobe and began taking out clothes.

'You, too, Dr. Watson.'

'No, no. I assure you ...' I began, but Holmes interrupted, and I was surprised by the wistfulness of his tone, as he said, 'Not quite so soon as you think.'

She stopped in front of him, her arms full of clothes.

'It's so funny. I asked for this assignment, you know.'

'Did you?'

'I was intended to go to Japan, but when I heard your name mentioned I could not resist the challenge of coming up against the best. I am sorry I didn't give you a closer game, Mr. Holmes.'

'We all have our setbacks,' he said gently. 'Though Dr. Watson never writes about mine.'

They stood looking at each other for some moments before she moved on to continue her packing. Holmes turned to see me standing there.

'Watson, if you would kindly do as I have suggested...'

'Dash it, Holmes... I...'

'If you are going to stand there swearing I shall have to summon the manager. Now hurry along, like a good fellow, or you will miss the explanation of it all.'

'The exp...' I started hopefully. He waved his hand. I followed its direction to his dressing-table. On it lay his folding telescope. I nodded to them both and hurried off to pack my things.

I was back in less than an hour. Bright sunlight now flooded their room, although it was still early. In my eagerness, I tripped over Ilse von Hoffmannsthal's bag, which she had set in the middle of the room, her parasol leaning against it. She herself was standing before a mirror, carefully adjusting her hat. She smiled at me, for all the world as if she had triumphed in the affair and could afford us her pity, instead of *vice versa*. I nodded and looked for Holmes. He was on the balcony, his telescope trained upon the loch.

'Holmes,' I whispered as I reached his side. 'What about the door? Won't she escape?'

'I think not,' he replied abstractedly.

'What are you looking for?'

'That.'

He handed over the telescope and gently turned me by the shoulders to face Urquhart Castle. I raised the glass to my eye. The framework of scaffolding was once more rising skyward. I lowered the telescope.

'What in heaven's name does it mean, Holmes? Those Trappists, or Germans, or whatever they are – they've got the submersible?'

'Yes, by now. They're about to sail it into the loch and make for the sea.'

'In *our* submersible! With *our* air pump! Holmes, I . . .'

'Do contain yourself. Just watch.'

I raised the glass again and could easily see the movement of the displaced water as the submersible slid from its subterranean lair into the deep loch. Our captive had joined us, and together we stood staring out across those silvery waters in which, only hours earlier, we had struggled and might have drowned. Suddenly, as though from an immense distance, there came the muffled thud of an explosion. All at once, some way ahead of where I had seen the waters move, there began a dreadful bubbling and foaming of the loch surface, and many little gouts of white water were shot upward, to fall back in spray which seethed like a scum on the boiling turbulence of the once-placid expanse.

I heard a little cry from the woman at my elbow, but did not look round. Fascinated and appalled, I continued to stare until, after a last great upheaval, the waters subsided into a tranquillity that showed no evidence of what had happened, save for a few small objects which floated where once there had been none. I lowered the glass and turned to Holmes.

'A champagne bottle, no doubt,' he remarked. 'Perhaps even a Bible. A strange combination to mark the end of a strange business.'

'If you wouldn't mind being a little less cryptic . . .' said I, determined this time to have the truth even if it meant assaulting him to get it. He must have recognized my determination.

'That was the last of H.M.S. *Jonah*,' he said. 'It would

seem that somebody carelessly loosened a few bolts. Our Trappists are by now in the eternal silence of the bottom of the loch.'

There was a knock at the door, and Mycroft Holmes entered, rubbing his hands and beaming.

'Did you see it, Sherlock?' he asked eagerly. 'Capital, capital! Fräulein von Hoffmannsthal?'

'Mr. Mycroft Holmes? I am ready.'

'If there is one thing I admire most about the Prussians it is their punctuality.'

'If there is one thing I do not admire about the British it is their climate,' rejoined our captive. 'I understand your jails are quite damp.'

'They are,' Mycroft nodded gravely. His face suddenly brightened. 'But you're not going to jail. You're going back to Germany.'

'Germany!'

'You will be conducted to the Swiss–German border, where you will be handed over in exchange for one of our agents – a man named Ibbetson.'

The beautiful young woman's eyes were radiant again. She turned to smile upon us all in turn, and I longed to tell her how glad I was; but, once again, I recalled that she had been our enemy, and no doubt would be again, and I kept silent.

'Thank you,' was all she said.

'Don't thank me,' Mycroft replied. 'Thank my brother. It was his idea.'

Her eyes and Holmes's met.

'Frankly,' Mycroft went on, 'I think we're making a very poor deal. You are much cleverer than most members of the British Secret Service – outside my own small branch, that is. Don't you agree, Sherlock?'

With a smile, Holmes gave his gallant little bow.

'And cleverer than some consulting detectives,' said he.

Mycroft signalled to the doorway, where I saw a man waiting. He came in and, with a nod to us, picked up Fräulein von Hoffmannsthal's bag. She stopped him and plucked the parasol from beneath the strap.

'I will take that,' she said; and then she and Mycroft and the man were gone, and Holmes and I were left together staring silently at the closed door.

'Holmes,' I said at length, clearing my throat, 'perhaps you'll give me all the details now?'

'What is there to add?' he replied. 'You have seen it all happen. It has worked itself out before you.'

'Nevertheless, as your biographer...'

'No, no. I don't believe she would care to have this story spread all over the pages of a popular magazine.'

'The public has a right to know these things, Holmes. Why should we concern ourselves about the feelings of a German spy?'

'I didn't mean Ilse von Hoffmannsthal,' he answered, moving towards the window. 'I meant Her Majesty the Queen.'

'Oh!'

I went to join him at the window. Beneath us, at the hotel entrance, the man carrying Ilse von Hoffmannsthal's bag was just about to heave it into an open carriage. Then she herself emerged, accompanied by Mycroft Holmes, who helped her into the carriage and got in beside her. The other man joined the driver on the seat and they went off at a smart pace, without any of them looking round.

As they went down the driveway, I saw Ilse von Hoffmannsthal open her parasol and raise it over her shoulder.

'Holmes,' I persisted, 'if I were to promise to include this amongst those cases which are not to be published in our lifetime...'

'Please be quiet,' he said. 'I am trying to read a message.'

I followed his gaze. For the last time the parasol was fluttering open and shut, unnoticed by Mycroft who sat stolidly looking out across the loch.

'What is she saying, Holmes?'

He did not answer until the parasol had fluttered its last.

'*Auf wiedersehen.*'

I stared at him, and then laughed.

'*Auf* ...! The nerve of the woman. I should have thought that of all people in the world she'd ever wish to see again, you'd be the last.'

He did not answer, but stayed as he was, staring and staring until the carriage had passed out of our sight. Even then he did not move until the last dust from its wheels had hung and then settled back on the road from which the swift passing had disturbed it.

EPILOGUE

Winter came swiftly that year. At one moment, it seemed, the trees in Regent's Park were ablaze with the dying embers of their glory; the next, they were bare, naked to the bitter wind which had stripped them of their raiment and flung it contemptuously about their feet. I remember waking one morning to notice something unaccustomed about my room, and then realizing what it was: the daylight was reflected upon the ceiling and high up the walls. A quick journey to the window confirmed my suspicion: Baker Street lay under a thick carpeting of snow. The early morning traffic had already reduced the roadway to the semblance of a mud bath, but everywhere else, on rooftops, walls, sills and pavements, the snow lay as pristine as it had fallen, giving strange brightness to a day of dull, cold cloud and whining wind.

I stood for some time admiring the novelty with which overnight snowfall invests the city scene, pitying the few pedestrians who struggled past, heavily muffled and clutching their clothing about them as they plodded and slid and panted against the cold. The scrape of spades told me that a few zealous householders and tradespeople were already at work to clear their steps and pavements, but otherwise there lay that unnatural quiet which a great city only knows when snow muffles hooves and wheels and drives half its population off its streets.

I turned away thankfully to enjoy another half-hour in

the warmth of my bed. Mrs. Hudson, I knew, would already be up and about, kindling fires and cooking stove, putting on water to boil, making all snug and warm in readiness for Holmes and myself to take our seats at the breakfast table. It was good, in that moment, to reflect that I need not venture forth all day, if I chose, and need make no closer acquaintance with the snow and slush than the view from our windows. I would remain in slippered ease and earn some welcome guineas by writing up my narratives of our most recent adventures.

Since the Loch Ness affair of that spring we had been little outside London. Holmes was always reluctant to leave the capital for any great length of time, feeling that to do so would be to embolden the criminal fraternity into increased activity. He preferred to sit, like a spider with his great web spun about him, awaiting the signal that would send him flying into action. Such signals were never infrequent. They would come at any hour of the day or night in the form of a letter, a messenger, a visit from a Cabinet Minister or a veiled lady. As his chronicler, it was my privilege to run at his heels upon the mysterious and often exciting errands which these summonses set in train; and thus it was that life at Baker Street comprised that most satisfying blend of contrasting existences, stimulating action of a sort to stretch a man's mental and physical capabilities, and the comfortable leisure that is the sweeter for having been well earned.

With such agreeable sentiments stirring in my mind, I joined Holmes at the table a little later and proceeded to make my usual hearty inroads into the plentiful fare which Mrs. Hudson had provided. We spoke little while eating, preferring to reserve our opinions for the after-breakfast pipe, and I was half-way through my second newspaper when Mrs. Hudson brought in the second delivery of post. There was none for me, but the usual assortment for

Holmes, which he rapidly went through, tossing most aside with an impatient snort, lingering intently upon anything which carried the slightest promise of a challenge to his powers.

'Hmm!' he exclaimed suddenly, evidently surprised. 'A letter from the Diogenes Club.'

'Perhaps,' said I, 'Mycroft is putting you up for membership.'

'If he is,' replied Holmes, slitting the envelope, 'it will only be to give himself the pleasure of blackballing his own brother.'

I watched him unfold the single sheet of paper and begin to read it, his eyes darting in their usual restless manner, impatient to seek out the kernel of the message. Then, all at once, I knew that something was amiss. His eyes had stopped moving and were focused as though upon one sentence, or word, even, of what he had read; and the expression in them was one which I did not associate with him.

Holmes turned the paper over and read something on the reverse. Then he rose slowly to his feet, placed the letter before me without comment, and went to stand staring down from the window at the wintry scene. I picked up the sheet of notepaper and read.

The Diogenes Club
Pall Mall
London W.

9th December

Dear Sherlock,

My sources in Tokyo inform me that Ilse von Hoffmannsthal was arrested last week by the Japanese counter-intelligence service for spying on naval installations in Yokohama harbour. After a secret trial she was summarily executed by firing squad.

I turned the note over. There was only one more sentence.

It might interest you to know that she had been living in Japan for these past months under the name of Mrs. Ashdown.

*Yours,
Mycroft.*

I looked towards Holmes. He was still standing with his back to the room, looking into the street. I rose to my feet.

'Holmes, I'm terribly sorry. I think I know how you feel.'

He said nothing. I was very much aware of the hushed street noises and could quite clearly hear a cab stopping outside our house and the slam of its door. The sound of our bell was strangely loud. A few moments later there came a tap at our door. I glanced inquiringly at Holmes. Without looking at me he strode to his bedroom and shut the door behind him.

'Come in,' I called.

The door opened and Inspector Lestrade peered round it.

'Good morning, Dr. Watson,' he greeted me cheerily. 'I just happened to be in the neighbourhood, and I thought . . .'

'What is it this time?' I asked.

'We've had three rather nasty murders in Whitechapel. All women. Very nasty. Some of us at the Yard were wondering if perhaps Mr. Holmes would be willing to step across and . . .'

'I'm sorry, Lestrade,' I interrupted him, 'Holmes is . . . working on another case just now.'

'Oh ... Too bad. I just thought it was the kind of thing that would interest him. Well, never mind. I daresay we can solve it without his help.'

'I daresay you can.'

He hesitated for a moment, then, with a nod, returned to the door. As he laid his hand upon the knob we heard, from Holmes's room, the first notes of that wistful Tschaikowsky melody. Lestrade turned to me inquiringly.

'Good day, Lestrade,' I said, and ushered him firmly out.

I closed the door and stood against it for some moments, listening to those infinitely romantic, infinitely sad phrases, then I went across to my chair beside our glowing fire, reached across to the desk for some sheets of paper and my pen and ink, and started to write this narrative.